KU-312-141

THE PALACE OF GOLD

Hilary Wilde

CHIVERS

| British Library Cataloguing in Publication Data available |

This Large Print edition published by AudioGO Ltd, Bath, 2013.
Published by arrangement with the Author

U.K.   Hardcover   ISBN   978 1 4713 0637 2
U.K.   Softcover   ISBN   978 1 4713 0638 9

Copyright © Hilary Wilde 1973

All rights reserved

Printed and bound in Great Britain by
MPG Books Group Limited

F 20806701 X 1 234

PEV   PLYMOUTH LIBRARY SERVICES

Please return or renew this book
by the latest date stamped below

WITHDRAWN
FROM
PLYMOUTH LIBRARIES

'Love converts the hut into a palace of gold'

CHAPTER ONE

Jean was in the kitchen when her flatmate, Maggie, called out: 'Just listen to this, Jean. The nerve of it!'

A tall girl with a cloud of dark hair, Jean took her hands from the soapy water and went to the doorway, sighing a little, for Maggie had been on edge all morning as they packed her suitcases for her holiday.

Waving a newspaper, Maggie, her corn-coloured hair piled high, her lovely face angry, went on: 'Men!' in a disgusted way. 'Whatever will they think of next? Listen to this advert, Jean. "A strong, healthy, energetic, cheerful young woman required,"' Maggie read aloud, frowning as she looked through the green-rimmed glasses she only wore when she read. '"Required to take charge of three children and housekeep a farm in Swaziland. Courage, good temper and common sense also needed as there are crocodiles at the bottom of the garden. Write Box . . . "' She looked up. 'I ask you, Jean, what does he want? A saint or a slave?'

Jean pushed back her dark hair and dried her hands on a tissue.

'Where is Swaziland?'

'I haven't a clue.' Maggie looked at the large trendy watch on her wrist. 'Dad's late. I hope we won't miss the plane.'

'You've got bags of time, Maggie. Your father never lets you down,' Jean said, and was worried by the wistful note in her voice, for she had never discussed her parents and their lack of love for her with Maggie, though maybe Maggie, having known her since they were at school together, could see it and realised that Jean preferred not to talk about it. 'I hope you have a lovely time in Majorca,' she added.

Maggie gave a little dance round the room in her white trouser suit. 'You bet I will!' she said happily.

Of course she would, Jean was thinking, for Maggie was one of those lucky *natural* girls who made friends wherever they went and enjoyed every experience. So different from Jean, with her five foot eleven inches to worry her, and the habit of stumbling over and knocking things down as well as her shyness when she met strangers. Maybe that was why her family had no time for her. They were ashamed of her because she was so different from their other two children—Reg, brilliantly clever, and Celia, just reaching seventeen and looking lovelier every day and knowing it, the lucky girl.

They heard a car and Jean helped carry Maggie's luggage down the steep narrow stairs to the street where her father and the huge red Jaguar were waiting.

'Goodbye, have a good time!' Jean called,

standing on the pavement and waving her hand.

She went upstairs slowly; the cold emptiness of the flat hit her almost physically as she went inside and closed the door. She switched on the transistor, for any noise was better than the terrible silence.

Wandering round the room, she tidied up as she thought back, wondering if she had made a mistake in coming to live in London. She had always lived at home in the Isle of Man until the year before. She had had a good job as a doctor's receptionist, but always dreaded the moment when she must go home at the end of the day. Then Maggie, who worked in London for a travel agency, had come on holiday and persuaded her to break away from home and share a flat in London. It had seemed exciting and the answer to Jean's problem, and she had expected a family argument. It was odd, but she had been both surprised and hurt to realise how glad her parents were that she was going. They could not wait to see the last of her, she thought bitterly as she pounded a cushion and looked round the drably-furnished room that Maggie had brightened with gay posters and coloured cushions. Despite Jean's dreams and Maggie's promises, London hadn't proved much better, as Jean had made few friends and hated her job in a typing pool, high in a huge building in Trafalgar Square.

'The answer is marriage,' Maggie had said

3

gaily one day when Jean confessed her hatred of her job. 'Obviously you need a husband and kids.'

Jean had smiled, hoping Maggie had not seen the shudder she gave. Even now she shivered, remembering those dreadful days when she could hear her parents quarrelling, hurling cruel words at one another that had made her think that if that was marriage, then it wasn't for her!

Jean picked up the newspaper Maggie had tossed on the floor, remembering what Maggie had read aloud. It took quite a while to find the advertisement, then she curled up in an armchair, kicked off her sandals, flicked some dust from her blue denim trews and looked at the paper.

She read the words aloud slowly, her dark eyes puzzled. What sort of job could this be? What sort of man if he was demanding the impossible?

Yet was it so *impossible* when you came to think of it?

'A strong, healthy, energetic, cheerful young woman . . .' Jean read slowly. Was that really asking too much, for a healthy girl would surely be energetic, and if she was energetic she would have lots of interesting hobbies, so that would make her cheerful.

Jean took a deep breath and read on: '. . . to take charge of three children and housekeep a farm in Swaziland.'

4

Well, that wasn't so bad. Three children . . . of course it would depend on their age. Housekeep . . . what exactly did that mean? Organising others to do the work? Or scrubbing floors and doing the washing for all the family? Maybe it would be a tough job, but . . .

Swaziland . . . Swaziland. She kept saying the word over and over again, letting it slide along her tongue. Where on earth was Swaziland?

She read on:

'Courage, good temper and common sense also needed.' Well, she thought aloud, tossing her dark hair that would slide forward over her face, that was fair enough. Courage—certainly that was needed in a strange land, but then whoever applied for the job would surely know that? Good temper? That too was right. Who wanted a bad-tempered nurse-housekeeper? Common sense? Just what was common sense? Not imagining things, perhaps—not being afraid of things that weren't actually there . . . in other words, not screaming that she saw a snake when it was the shadow of a wind-blown leaf?

Now why had he put: 'because there are crocodiles at the bottom of the garden'? It was almost as if he wanted to frighten would-be applicants. Crocodiles . . . surely that gave a clue? What countries in the world had crocodiles in their gardens?

South America? The Amazon? Or was that alligators? She jumped up, crossing the square room with the window looking out on roof tops and Battersea's tall chimneys, then looked in the cupboard where Maggie kept a mass of books. At last she found what she was looking for—an atlas. The countries were marked with Maggie's ink as she planned all the places she hoped to visit one day. Luckily there was an index at the end.

'Ah!' Jean exclaimed happily as she saw the number of the page and the cross numbers. She opened the book at the right page, lying on the floor, her long slender body curled up like a sleeping cat's, as she looked in search of the unknown Swaziland.

'There!' she said triumphantly, her finger finding the small circular country. It was close to Mozambique. It sounded exciting, unusual, even . . . even romantic. Swaziland was above South Africa and far below Rhodesia. It looked terribly small. What sort of country would it be?

Back to the cupboard she went, hunting through Maggie's books, but she could find nothing about Swaziland. Glancing at the clock, she saw the library would still be open, so she hastily flung on her anorak —for although it was the end of May there was a cold wind outside—and hurried to the local library.

A blank stare met her question in there, for

no one seemed to have heard of Swaziland, but then one assistant coming up to join them laughed.

'I know a lot about Swaziland. My sister's mother-in-law went out to her son's wedding.'

'What sort of place is it?' Jean asked eagerly.

'She loved it. Said it was like the Lake District only there were no lakes. Several dams, but, she said, they were different. She liked it very much. She called it a gracious way of living.' The red-headed assistant laughed. 'Sounded a bit too out-of-this-world for my liking. It was a British Protectorate, you know.'

'I don't know,' Jean confessed. 'I've never heard of it before.'

'Well, now it's an independent country and everything is fine. Only one tribe, one language and one king. She loved it there, as I said. Lots of sunshine, beautiful mountains . . .'

'And . . . and the people?'

'Very friendly. A good social life, she said. No transport, though. That was one big snag if you hadn't a car.'

'I see.' Jean hesitated, not sure why she was asking these questions and yet feeling she had to know more about the small isolated country. 'Did she see any crocodiles?'

'Several, and lots of snakes and mosquitoes.' The red-headed assistant laughed. 'Not for me. Give me London any day!' She turned away, and Jean hurried home.

7

It sounded almost fantastic and out of this world. The flatlet was as quiet and cold as earlier that day. Automatically Jean switched on Maggie's television set, given her by an adoring father.

Maybe she should wash her hair, she thought, and went to the bathroom. She was just rubbing the thick dark hair with a towel when something on the television caught her attention. It was a woman's voice, amused, sarcastic and perhaps a little malicious. 'You're asking too much of any woman, Mr. Crosby,' she said. 'Crocodiles at the bottom of the garden? You're either joking or . . .'

'I am not joking,' a deep masculine voice answered.

With the towel twisted round her head, Jean almost stumbled in her haste and stood in the bathroom doorway staring at the TV screen.

An elegant, rather supercilious-looking girl was staring at a tall, lean man. He was smiling.

'I assure you there are crocodiles at the bottom of the garden,' he said, his voice amused. 'Naturally they are avoided, as they are not good friends. Why do you say I'm asking too much of any woman? After all, a job is just a job.'

Jean went to sprawl on the rug before the box, fascinated. Normally she was not interested in men, a weakness that had often worried her, but suddenly she found herself staring at this man as if he was someone she had been looking for all her life. No one could call him handsome, she told herself. But his blond, slightly reddish hair was long, not very long but just resting on his collar with a natural curl. He had a lean face and amused eyes. He was well-dressed but not trendy at all. A well-cut dark suit and a pale pink shirt. Now he smiled, and his face seemed to light up.

'As I said, a job is a job,' he told the suddenly silent girl sitting by his side.

'Just exactly what do you want her to do? Couldn't you find someone in Swaziland to do the job? I mean, why do you want an English girl?'

'I want an English girl because . . .' he began, then suddenly there was a flashing of quivering lights on the screen and it went into darkness.

'Oh, no!' Jean murmured as she went to the set and tried to get the picture and sound back. It had happened to the set before and she would have to send for a mechanic on Monday. She waited, hoping the impossible would happen, but of course it didn't. At last she gave up hope, switched off and went to the kitchen to whip up a couple of eggs and make some toast.

Why had the TV set to behave like that? Just as it was getting really interesting. What was the man's name? Crosby . . . that was it, Jean was thinking as she worked; carefully watching the toaster, because that, too, could be temperamental and there wasn't much bread. She should have gone shopping that day, but she had helped Maggie iron her dresses and pack her cases, so they had been too busy to think of it.

Why had he wanted an English girl? What was his answer going to be? And . . . well, he didn't seem the sort of man to waste money on an advertisement just for a joke, did he? she asked herself.

After she had eaten, listening to the radio and yet not really hearing it, Jean couldn't forget the short frustrating scene. If only the set could have lasted a little longer! What *was* his reason for wanting an English girl? And what sort of life would it be . . . how old were the three children? What kind of farm was it? Would she . . . Jean's hand flew to her mouth. Would *she*, she had thought. So was that why she was so interested in it? Had she already, subconsciously, of course, made up her mind to apply for the job?

She almost swept the dirty plates in the tiny sink and went to sit by the window, looking at the chimney pots as twilight slowly approached.

'You must be mad!' she told herself. 'Why, you've had no experience with children and know nothing about farming.'

But you could learn, a little voice inside her said softly. And think of going to a beautiful place like Swaziland. Think of going far away

10

from your home . . . think how startled the family would be. Perhaps they'd miss you. Why not apply for the job? the little voice persisted.

'Nonsense,' Jean told herself, jumping up. She'd have a bath and an early night and she wouldn't think of it again!

That night she dreamt of it! It wasn't a pleasant dream, she thought sleepily as she woke up, for she had run miles and miles up and down mountains with two crocodiles chasing her!

The day dragged as lonely Sundays always did. Most of the other flat tenants seemed to be out. Jean tried to find odd things to do, but her thoughts went back again and again.

'A job is a job,' he had said.

What did he mean? A job is a job? Did he mean that no matter where you were, it was a *job* and so you accepted it without . . . what was the word? oh yes, *dispute*. Or should it be *questioning*? Well, he was right in a way. After all, he was being quite honest—telling them the hard parts of it rather than the good.

He'd surely get lots of answers to his advertisement, even more as a result of his television appearance. If only . . . if only the wretched set hadn't broken down, Jean kept thinking.

On Monday she awoke early and got up. It was pelting with rain. Of course in Africa the sun would be shining. It was always shining in countries like Africa, she thought, shivering

11

a little as she got out her boots and green mackintosh. Glancing at the clock, she saw she was much too early, and suddenly she did what she had subconsciously known she would do all along. She opened the newspaper she had tossed in a corner, then sat down by Maggie's typewriter. 'Dear Sir,' she wrote, 'I am afraid I have had no experience with children nor with farming, but I am strong, healthy, energetic and usually cheerful. I think I have courage, I know I have a good temper, because I hate scenes, and I'm sure I have common sense. I'm not sure what I'd do if a crocodile chased me—I think I'd run! Swaziland sounds marvellous and I'm eager to get out of England as soon as I can. I'm twenty-two, five foot eleven inches tall, fond of tennis, badminton, and I can play a little golf. I also swim and . . .' Carefully she crossed out the last word *and*, then put a full stop instead. She finished:

'I would like to apply for the job. I am working in a typing pool so could only come for an interview in the evening or the weekend.'

She signed it quickly, her eyes skimming over the work, then she hunted in the mess that was Maggie's desk and found a stamp. She'd drop it in the letter box on her way to work . . . send it off before she lost courage and tore up the letter.

She hurried down the stairs and out into the

bleak cold wet day, the wind bringing the rain against her skin, shivering as she waited for the bus that always seemed to be late. One thing, *that* would be no problem in Swaziland—because in Swaziland there were no buses at all.

The bus came in sight, weaving its way with incredible skill through the cars. As Jean jumped on it quickly, her more sensible, square side scolded her:

'You've done the stupidest thing of your life. You haven't a single qualification. I doubt very much if you'll even get an answer.'

The funny thing was the voice inside her sounded just like her father's: impatient, exasperated, then sympathetic because she was the stupid one of the family.

*   *   *

The days dragged by. Jean waited, not sure if she really wanted an answer, as the postman brought no reply to her letter. It wouldn't have been so bad had she had Maggie there or even had someone with whom she could talk, but there was no one at all. At the office, some of the girls had seen the advert and the TV interview, but they saw it as a huge joke.

'After what he'd said about the farm, who'd want to go there? Like being buried alive,' one girl said.

Another laughed, 'I think it's all a big joke.

No man like Peter Crosby would stand for it. He'd send the kids to boarding school, that's more like it—men like Peter Crosby haven't time for children.'

Jean had listened, aching to ask the reason he had given for wanting an English girl, yet she hesitated, afraid her clumsy way of putting things might betray what, to them, would be worse than crazy: she had applied for the job.

Why had she done it? she kept asking herself. Why? He would have answers from so many fully qualified people, she hadn't a chance . . . And even if she had . . . Her mind was a turmoil of contradictory thoughts.

When the, letter came she couldn't believe her eyes. She was late that morning and snatched it up from the table in the hall by the front door and hurried down the street, opening the letter as she went. It was curt and impersonal. 'Mr. Crosby will see you on Saturday at three-fifteen,' was all it said, giving an address in Belgravia.

Jean nearly missed the bus as she thrust the letter into her handbag, and running, leapt on at the last moment. Inside she stood, swaying with the bus, and feeling dazed. It couldn't be true. He had written to her. He was going to interview her!

Suddenly a wave of horror swept through her. Was she mad? she asked herself. What sort of job could it be if he was unable to get a fully qualified person—if he had to turn to someone like herself who had so little to offer?

She was glad it was Friday, so she wouldn't have long to wait—but should she bother to go? Or perhaps write a polite note apologising and saying she could no longer apply for the job? It was a difficult day as the hands of the clock seemed to crawl while she sat at her typewriter, making the most stupid, unforgivable typing errors, listening silently as the superintendent, Mrs. Callow, scolded her at first and then asked anxiously if she was all right.

'You look very odd,' she said.

Jean managed to laugh. 'I'm fine . . . just a bit . . . '

'Dreamy? In love, I suppose.' The little old woman with snow-white hair and a slight limp smiled, shaking her head. 'How it messes up your work!'

'I'm not in love . . .' Jean began, then the words seemed to dwindle away into nothing. Of course she wasn't in love, she told herself angrily. How could she be in love with a man who she had seen on television for a few minutes? It was absurd even to think of it.

That night she carefully washed and set her hair, then looked through her wardrobe, wondering what sort of impression she should give. Not too trendy but not too square, surely?

Not that it really mattered in the end, because next day it was pelting with rain, the streets awash with water, the trees bending their branches under the heavy downfall. Keeping an anxious eye on the clock, for men like Peter Crosby would value punctuality more than her appearance, she felt sure, Jean wore a cream jersey dress and her green mackintosh. It *would* rain, of course, to spoil her hair but she hunted out a rainhood and put it on carefully. Maybe it would keep her hair tidy, she thought, and that would be a change.

She got to the address in Belgravia fifteen minutes too early, so, despite the rain, she walked round, glancing up at the posh hotel where Peter Crosby was living. At last the time came and she went inside. The entrance hall was lofty and brilliantly bright with red and gold decor. The receptionist looked at her oddly as Jean asked for Mr. Crosby.

'His suite is on the second floor,' she said with a smile. 'There's a cloakroom just round the corner where you can leave your mackintosh.'

'Thanks,' Jean said with a quick nervous smile. She wondered how many girls had come to be interviewed by Mr. Crosby. Her hand was shaking as she took off the rainhood and combed her hair. It looked slightly squashed, but that was better than its usual tangles. Quickly she made up, found the cloakroom attendant and dropped a silver coin into the waiting saucer that was filled with silver coins, then hurried to the lift.

She saw it was one of those lifts that are like boxes that never move, and this didn't help her at all, because she wanted to scream as the door closed and nothing happened. Suppose it broke down, suppose . . .? The door opened slowly and, still trembling, she stepped outside. Why was she here? she suddenly wondered. The temptation to turn and flee was great, but at that moment the door facing her opened and a tall lean man stood there. Jean recognised him immediately.

'Miss Hamilton?' he asked, and when she nodded, he opened the door still wider and said: 'Please come in. Not a very pleasant day, I'm afraid.'

It was obviously a sitting-room with the closed door of another room at the other end, luxuriously furnished with dark green carpet, and there were gold-streaked pink curtains.

'Please sit down,' he said.

As she sank into one of the deep armchairs, feeling as if she was being swallowed and wishing she had chosen another one, he jerked a hard-backed chair round and straddled it, resting his elbows on the back of the chair, and his chin on his hands as he looked at her.

'Why did you apply for the job?' he asked bluntly.

'Why? I . . . well . . .' Jean swallowed nervously and then decided to tell the truth. 'It . . . it intrigued me. I'd never heard of Swaziland, and . . .'

'Yet, in your letter, you admitted that you would run away if you saw a crocodile. Suppose one of the children were there?'

She tried to sit up, but every movement she made seemed to draw her deeper into the armchair. 'That would be different.'

'I see. Your courage would react to the situation.'

'Of course it would!' she began indignantly, then stopped. 'I'm sure it would,' she added more uncertainly.

'Your letter was frank. What made you think you could be suitable for the job when you have no qualifications?'

'I don't know why I applied, but something made me.'

'Something?' His voice rose. 'What is something?'

She twisted her hands together, looking at them to avoid meeting his eyes, cold hard eyes that seemed able to pierce into her mind. She knew she could never lie to him, for he would always know.

'I was feeling lonely and miserable. My flatmate had gone to Majorca with her parents and I'd just had a letter from my mother, suggesting that I didn't go home for my holiday as she didn't know if they'd be there.'

'In other words, you and your family don't get on?'

She looked at him. 'We do . . . on the surface. But I know . . . I know I'm a

18

disappointment to them. You see, Reg—he's my brother and older than me, is brilliant and has a wonderful job. I failed all my exams. Then there's Celia, she's just seventeen and they're awfully proud of her, because she's really lovely.'

'Why shouldn't they be proud of you?'

Jean swallowed. 'Because . . . because I haven't ever done anything to make them proud of me.'

'How come?'

'I don't know.' She spread out her hands as if imploring for an answer. 'I've tried, I've tried ever so hard. I studied and studied and studied. I'm just stupid. Then I'm so tall . . .'

A flicker of a smile went over his face. 'I noticed that. What is there to be ashamed of in being tall? I'm taller than you and it doesn't worry me.'

'But you're a man.' She stared at him. 'Can't you see, when a girl's too tall, she looks . . .'

'Beautiful,' he said. 'If she'll let herself look like that. Of course, if you go creeping round, your shoulders hunched up, your head sticking out like an ostrich's . . .'

Jean's hand went to her mouth as her eyes widened. That was something her mother was always on at her about.

'Do I look like that?' she asked.

'Sometimes,' he said, 'but not always. So you are, I take it, the middle child.' He smiled when she nodded. 'It's never easy for them. I

19

was lucky. I was the eldest. I have a younger brother in Australia and my sister . . .' It was as if a cloud closed down over his face and his voice, even, seemed to retreat as he went on: 'My sister and her husband died nearly a year ago, in a car crash. They lived in Swaziland, had a farm there. My mother moved in to look after the children. There's a manager for the farm. I thought she would enjoy it, she's always saying how lonely she is, but apparently I was wrong. She wrote to me recently, when I came back from lecturing in America, and I was shocked to learn that her health was not so good and she found the children too much of a handful. Strictly speaking, they're my wards, because my sister appointed me their guardian. This means I must go and live in Swaziland to free my mother from her position.'

'But your work?'

The smile flicked again, if it could be called a smile. His voice was grave. 'Fortunately for me I can fit it in. I've been commissioned to write a series of books and Swaziland is a quiet place where I could get my work done. That is . . .' he gave another funny smile, 'if the kids are quiet.'

'It isn't natural for children to be quiet . . .' she began.

He frowned and his voice had a hard edge to it. 'They'll have to learn if they want to live with me.'

There was a sudden ringing of a phone bell. He stood up. 'I'm expecting a long-distance call. You'll excuse me?' He walked rapidly across the room to the other door, closing it behind him.

Jean seized the chance to wriggle and pull herself out of the deep armchair and look around the room for another one, in which she could sit with more dignity. She chuckled— hark at her! Thinking of *dignity*, but it was very embarrassing to keep sliding deeper and deeper into the chair.

Looking round her, she found another one, one she could sit in, knowing she could rise at any moment. Glancing at the furniture, she noticed another phone. So Mr. Crosby could have answered the phone from this room, she thought. Probably it was someone he wanted to talk to privately. His girl-friend? He obviously wasn't married, but surely no man so attractive could stay a bachelor for ever?

But was he really attractive? He was a strange man, changing his voice all the time; one moment friendly and understanding, the next curt and cold. His face, too. No one could call him handsome, and when he frowned his face seemed to cloud and darken—but one of his rare smiles seemed to brighten it instantly. Let's say, she thought, that he wasn't attractive but fascinating. No, that was too strong a word. Interesting, perhaps.

The door opened and he came back.

'Sorry about that. I see you found that chair rather overwhelming.'

She felt herself relax. 'I felt I was being swallowed,' she explained.

He chuckled. 'I know. Now where were we? Oh yes. I was telling you about Swaziland. Do you know anything about it?'

'I'd never heard of it, so I looked it up in an atlas. Also someone at the library told me her sister's mother-in-law, I think it was, had been out there to her son's wedding She liked it very much—called it gracious living.'

Peter Crosby threw back his head and laughed. Jean was quite startled. What was there funny about that? When he stopped, he looked serious.

'I don't want you to get the wrong idea, Miss Hamilton. Swaziland is a small country, about as big as Wales. It's very mountainous. The Swazis are a pleasant people, good-tempered, proceeding fast since they had Independence, but where we're going to live . . .' He paused as if he had noticed the surprise on her face at his use of the word *we*, and added, almost angrily: '. . . I mean the children and I, of course, is a very remote part of Swaziland. We're five miles from the main road and in the wet season often it's almost impossible to get down the track that leads to the farm. All is well if the tractors are running, but they're always breaking down. The house itself, I understand, is pretty primitive in many ways. My brother-in-law was a talker, he was always going to build on rooms or modernise it. I haven't met the manager, though my mother likes him. Not that that means anything, because she likes the strangest of people.' He chuckled. 'Actually she's been trying to get a governess-help out there, but all the girls want to go to the cities, and I don't blame them. It sounds pretty ghastly. Ninety miles from a train, twenty miles from the nearest town, if it could be called one, with a few stores and several garages and, of course, a hotel.'

He paused, and Jean seized her opportunity. 'You've been there?'

'No, never.'

'Then how do you know what it's like?'

His face relaxed into a smile. 'A good question—and clever expertise. I know nothing about Swaziland, either, except what my sister wrote in her letters. She hated it.'

'But someone else might enjoy living there? This old lady . . .'

'Quite. The point is this: could you enjoy that sort of isolation? True, there is some social life, playing bridge and drinking coffee. You're very keen on getting the job, aren't you?' He suddenly threw the question at her as if it was a knife.

Startled, she told the truth. 'I'm not sure.'

'Why did you apply for it, then? Are you wasting my time?'

'I do want it—and yet I don't.'

'I see.' He folded his arms. 'Give me the reasons *why* you want it. An escape from your family?'

She twisted her hands together. 'I honestly don't know. I was feeling pretty down the day you put in the advert,' she began and, to her amazement, found herself telling this stranger exactly what had happened. Maggie's impatience as she waited for her father to fetch her, glancing through the newspaper and seeing the advert, coming to the kitchen to ask Jean what this man wanted: a saint or a slave. 'Then she went, and it was so quiet and lonely,' Jean confessed, twisting her fingers together as she spoke, not looking at him. 'And . . . and I read the advertisement. It made sense to me.'

'In what way?' he asked quietly.

'Well, a job of governess to young children would require all the qualities you asked for— common sense, good temper, good health, etcetera. Then Swaziland sounded so unusual and I looked it up on the map, as I told you, then I went to the library to see if I could find anything about it.'

'Your interest was caught. I suppose because you were bored.'

'I wasn't bored.' She looked up quickly. 'I was . . . I envied Maggie her parents who think she's super, I envied her the trip to Majorca. I had no idea where to go for a holiday on my own.'

'Your boy-friends?'

24

She looked at him. 'I have none.' She found herself smiling. 'Maggie says I'm no career girl, that I should marry and have children, but . .'

'But you don't like men?' He sounded amused, so she looked at him.

'I do and I don't. I think the truth is, I'm scared of marriage.'

He grinned. 'That makes two of us. Why are you?'

She sighed. 'Well, maybe I shouldn't tell this to a stranger or anyone, but my parents are always fighting, having terrible arguments in which they say the most awful things and then, next day, they're laughing and joking as if nothing had happened. If people said those sort of things to me, I'd never forget them.'

'Some people find quarrels refreshing, they enjoy the reconciliations so much.'

'I wouldn't. Would you?' She looked him in the face and he stared back at her, a strange expression in his eyes.

'No, I wouldn't,' he agreed. 'So you were feeling depressed and this advert interested you. Right?'

'Yes . . . but the funniest thing happened. I knew I could never get the job, so I forgot it. Then when I got back from the library I turned on the television and you were being interviewed.'

'That's one way of putting it. She wanted to cut me up into strips—a real Women's Lib advocate! What did you think of it?'

Jean leaned forward, moving her hands expressively.

'That was the maddening part. You were just going to say why you wanted an English governess and the telly packed up. I was mad!'

Peter Crosby was smiling. 'I can imagine. So you never heard my description of the farm with the snakes in the long grass, the bulls wandering round, the mosquitoes eating you and . . .'

'The crocodiles at the bottom of the garden? think it was that sentence that fascinated me. I can't imagine it. Is it true?'

'Absolutely—according to my sister. Sometimes small piccanins playing in the water get caught or their mothers, washing the clothes in the river, get drawn in. I gather people are apt to forget the dangers that lie hidden. So you decided to apply for the job?'

'No, I knew it was useless. You see, I failed all my exams and . . . and . . .'

'Yet you applied?'

She fidgeted, unhappy as he looked at her. 'I know. I just couldn't make up my mind then on Monday, just before I went to work.' She told him how she found it was too early, so wrote the letter. 'I never expected an answer. You must have had lots of applicants,' she finished.

He leaned back, stretching his legs. 'I did, a great many, but I'm afraid what I told them put most of them off. Have I put you off?' He spoke so seriously that Jean was surprised and hesitated before answering.

'No, I don't think so.'

'Why not?'

'Well . . .' She moved her head and her hair swung forward, covering her face so she had to push it back with both hands, as she looked at him. 'Sorry, my hair is like me—clumsy and a nuisance.'

'I think it's beautiful hair,' he told her, his voice impersonal as if he was talking about a flower in a garden. 'Go on. Why haven't I put you off?'

'Well, first you've never been out there yourself and your sister might have had other reasons for being unhappy, so used the country as . . .'

'A whipping boy?' He nodded. 'A clever thought. Go on.'

'Then . . . then I've never been really abroad. I mean, I've been to the Continent, but not really *abroad*. Africa sounds . . . well, it sounds exciting.'

'Wait until the mosquitoes bite you!' he grinned.

'They do here.'

He chuckled. 'Right again. Go on.'

'Also . . . also I'd like to break right away, find a different way of living, become . . .'

'Yourself.' He nodded as if he understood. 'It's rather a chip on your shoulder, as they call it, isn't it? This feeling you have about your family. I mean, have you any real evidence that they don't love you?'

The phone bell shrilled. This time Peter Crosby went to the phone close by.

'What? Who? No, say I'm engaged . . . No. I don't know. Tell her I'm sorry, but I'll call her later. No, I can't say when.' There were strong notes of impatience and annoyance in his voice and Jean wondered who it was that wanted him to call her immediately. His girl-friend?

He returned to his chair, frowning.

'Well,' he said slowly, 'what were we talking about? Of course, your family. I take it you want to get away, become a real person, have a job you can be proud of, then later return, and have them welcome you with wide open arms.'

His sarcastic voice came as a surprise and Jean flinched. Was that why she wanted the job?

'I did think that if I went far away, they might . . .'

'Love you?' He stood up and began to walk round the room, hands clasped behind his back, a frown marring his face. 'Love isn't as easy to get as that. I would say you're quite wrong, that your parents love you and would show it if you gave them a chance. You're so convinced you're sort of a layabout . . . Look, you're an attractive girl; intelligent, sensible. What more can a parent ask? You're the one who's asking for the impossible. Distance doesn't overcome problems, it merely means

28

you're avoiding them. Best thing you could do is to go home and believe you're a someone, and then you will be.'

Jean stood up quickly. 'I'm . . .' She swallowed. How could he say such cruel things—even if they were true? Was she a coward—running away? Should she go back? 'I'm sorry I've wasted your time,' she finished.

He stood up, too, holding out his hand. 'You haven't wasted my time, nor is the interview ended. What you do with your life is your affair and not mine. Suppose I offer you the job, will you accept it?'

She stared, unable to believe him. 'You mean . . .?'

'I said *suppose*. Do you feel capable of handling the job? Able to live in a small community where gossip is the main hobby—according to my sister,' he added with a faint smile.

Sitting down again, she looked up at the tall man standing by her chair. 'I could try. Would I have to teach the children?'

'Heavens, no! They go to school—all three of them. It's someone to keep an eye on them when they're not at school that I want. Also to run the house, do the shopping, and so on. My sister had two very good house-girls who can, I understand, cook, and they've stayed on, despite my mother's rather perfectionist demands. There's also a laundry girl and two garden boys, Dorothy said in one of her letters that they had real green fingers. You wouldn't have any menial work to do,' Peter Crosby finished, his voice, Jean thought, condescending.

Her cheeks were hot. 'I wouldn't mind that. You really want someone to keep the children out of your way.'

Peter Crosby laughed. 'Right again. That's precisely what I do want. My sister and I were close friends, but she married a man I disapproved of. Unfortunately she wouldn't listen to me. I'm not saying their marriage was an unhappy one, but neither was it a happy one. Bill was absolutely nuts when it came to anything financial. That's another thing I've got to do . . . have a look at the books, for I gather from my mother that Bill left a lot of debts, so there isn't much for the children. The manager of the farm, a chap called Whitwell, seems to be struggling to do his best. You any good at figures?'

'Yes, that's about the only thing I am good at. Dad said I should be an accountant, but how can I when I just can't pass exams?'

'Well, you'll be useful to me, for there'll be hours when the kids are at school and you can help me.'

Jean caught her breath. Had he accepted her?

'I've had no experience with children,' she began, but Peter Crosby interrupted.

'Are you chickening out?'

'No, but . . . Are you serious? I mean, have I got the job?'

'Yes. Have I got you as an employee?'

Jean looked at her hands. She should have put some nail varnish on . . . did she want the job? Did she want to work for this strange man, one moment sympathetic, the next cruel, one moment smiling, the next scowling? Did she want to live in a lonely spot with no friends and three difficult children to keep quiet and an African staff to control when she couldn't speak their language?

But could she say *no* and never see him again?

She looked up at him. 'Yes,' she said.

He smiled. 'Good.' He glanced at his watch. 'Well, that's that. Look, I'll be in touch with you. You've got a passport? Good. Better go along to your doctor to make sure your vaccination is up-to-date, and there may be a few more injections needed——I must get my secretary to check about it. Give notice at your job and you'll hear from me. I should say we'll be off within the next month. We'll fly out . . . my secretary will arrange for the tickets and so on. Anyhow, I'll be in touch with you. Goodbye.'

He held out his hand and shook hers. Jean liked the firm warmth of his fingers. She walked to the door as in a daze, everything rather blurred.

'Miss Hamilton.' Peter Crosby's voice rang

31

loud and clear, stopping her instantly, making her turn round to look at him. He was walking towards her, a frown between his eyes.

'I've been thinking, Miss Hamilton,' he said. 'It would simplify matters considerably if you were my wife.'

'Your . . . wife?' she echoed.

He nodded. 'Don't look so horrified. It would be what they call a marriage of convenience, of course.'

It seemed a long time before Jean found her voice.

'A marriage of convenience?' she said slowly.

He nodded. 'It might be more convenient for us both.'

'But I hardly know you.'

He smiled then. 'We might get on better because of that. Come and sit down again. We must discuss it.'

Discuss it! Jean thought. What a cold-blooded way of describing it! Marry him? She could not believe it. He wanted to marry her. Had he, too, fallen in love at first sight, just as she had done when she saw him on the television?

Obediently she sat down while he got a chair as before and straddled it. Was he joking? she wondered, then realised that he was not. Indeed the reverse, for he kept rubbing his hand across his face as if puzzled. He talked, too, as if he was thinking aloud, having forgotten she was there.

'It's a small community where we shall be living. I've come across such in other countries. The wives have little or nothing to do but drink coffee and chatter. Gossip can begin quite reasonably as a shared interest in each other's problems, but it can also become malicious. A wife jealous of a younger woman—or angry because her neighbour's husband has got promotion. It's amazing what petty things can cause maliciousness to start. I can just hear them saying: "Have you heard that poor Bill's brother-in-law has come to live here and brought a young girl with him? Of course she's the children's *governess*," and then there would be laughter. I can just imagine the way they'd look at us when we go to the Club.'

'But . . . but . . .' Jean tried to break in. 'Surely people wouldn't think . . .'

Peter Crosby shook his head slowly. 'They certainly would. A young girl like you.'

'I'm twenty-two!'

'And you look about sixteen. Also I expect I've got a bit of a name as a womaniser. I got a great deal of publicity while in America. Not from choice, of course, but it seemed that every time I took a pretty girl out, the cameras caught me and there I would be on the front page. "English Professor of Social Economics escorting his latest girl-friend."' He gave a funny little laugh. 'You can be sure Dorothy will have seen some of those photos, because my mother collected them. Why, I don't know. Also . . .' he lifted his hand as he saw Jean was trying to speak, 'it might make it easier for you with the children. After all, an aunt is less formidable than a governess. The staff, too. No, I think it would be a good idea. We'll be crossing the border quite a lot, probably into Mozambique often, and we always have to fill in forms. Much simpler to scrawl "and wife".' He laughed. 'Not that that really matters, but all the same . . . Well,' his voice changed and became sharp, 'what do you think of the idea?'

Jean shook her head, trying to clear her mind, and her hair fell forward, screening her face. She was grateful for the moments it gave her to think as she pushed it back and looked at him.

'I think it's mad. If those people have such nasty minds . . .' she said, for what else could she think?

'You'd rather not take the job?'

She took a deep breath. So that was her choice, was it? The job and marriage, or refusal to many someone she didn't even know, and no job.

'My mother said in her letter that it was time I ceased to be a selfish bachelor—why she used the word selfish I can't think—and got married, so she'd be glad.' His face was grave, but there was amusement in his voice. Jean wondered why. None of it seemed funny to her.

'But marriage . . .' she said slowly.

'I know, but it isn't a real marriage,' he told her, his voice patient as if he was talking to a child. 'I know you feel about marriage just as I do, that there can be rows and unhappiness, but that wouldn't apply in this case. There'd be no romantic nonsense. You'd still be employed by me and I would pay your salary into your bank account each month. Of course I'll buy your clothes and we'll act in public like a happily married couple. I think we could be that—keeping it all on a businesslike level. A marriage of convenience.' He said the words as if he liked them.

Jean shivered. This was not her idea of marriage. Although she was afraid of it, she knew that she wanted to be married one day. But deep down inside her, a tiny bit of hope was born. A marriage of convenience would mean they would see a lot of one another, that in time he might grow to love her . . . and that then the word *convenience* could be dropped and they would be really married. If she walked out now she would never see him again and there would be no chance at all of marrying him. This way . . . this way, if she could make him love her . . .

'Yes,' she said quietly.

Peter Crosby nodded. 'Sensible girl! Now we must plan what we'll do. We'd better go up and meet your parents.'

'Oh no,' Jean said quickly, her face showing

her dismay. 'No, no, no! They'd . . .' She shivered as she thought of her mother asking questions. "How long have you known him? Isn't he too old for you? He must be nearly ten years older!" And her father would frown and say: "Aren't you rushing things? A six-month engagement is advisable." And in any case, would she be able to fool them? She was always so clumsy with the way she talked when at home, so she would probably give the whole thing away. She could imagine their remarks. 'Poor old Jean, making a fool of herself as usual!'

Peter Crosby glanced at his watch. 'I've just got to make a phone call and then I suggest we go out and have dinner and discuss this more slowly. I don't want to upset you, but I don't like us marrying without telling your parents.'

'I'm of age,' she pointed out.

'I know, but . . .' He stood up. 'I won't be long,' he said, and vanished into the bedroom.

Alone, she wandered round the room. Was she quite mad? Marrying a man she didn't know just for his convenience? But was it? she asked herself. What about hers?

There was a long mirror on the wall and she went to stand in front of it staring at her reflection and seeing a much too tall girl with a great mass of dark hair tumbling forward over her cheeks, a girl with dark unhappy eyes and a trembling mouth. What should she do? Was she being a fool? Was it her imagination that made her think she loved him? Was it possible to fall in love so suddenly? To love a man you didn't know.

Suddenly there was another reflection in the mirror—a tall man, taller than she by quite a few inches, a little smile on his face as he came closer and lifted her hair, twisted it round into a little bun on top and held it there, smiling at her.

'I like it best this way,' he said.

'I . . . I tried it once at a dance and it suddenly fell down. I nearly died of shame,' she confessed.

'And never tried it again? Typical of you!' He let go her hair so that it fell down to her shoulders. 'Ready? I'm hungry.'

'But it's not five yet.'

'I know, but I had no lunch. I eat when it suits me—not by set times. There's a nice little restaurant round the corner. We can have something to drink first.'

'I must just . . .' Jean began.

'Powder your nose? Nonsense, I like shiny noses. I hate the artificial look of today—coloured lids to eyes. I see you don't.'

She did usually, but she hadn't done them that day. Nor had she worn her false eyelashes, she thought thankfully.

Peter Crosby took her arm and chatted in a quiet friendly way as he led her to the door and down in the lift, waiting patiently while she collected her mackintosh.

It had stopped raining. Walking along the damp pavement, he smiled down at her.

'Know something, Jean? I think we could make a very good partnership.'

The tiny bit of hope began to grow. Perhaps she was doing the right thing after all. She looked up at him and thought how lovely it was to walk with a man taller than herself. She loathed walking with men she towered above and knew they must hate it, too.

'We can at least try,' she said hopefully.

CHAPTER TWO

Six weeks later, Jean was staring through the window of the plane down at the weird-looking country below. The plane seemed to be hardly moving and the ground was just like the television pictures of the surface of the moon. She felt sick with fear inside her as she sat very still, aware of the man by her side, completely ignoring her as he read through some notes he had taken out, of his dispatch case.

They had been married the day before, Maggie and Peter's secretary being the witnesses. Then they had driven straight out to Heathrow to board the plane that had brought them after a long sleepless night to Johannesburg where they had changed to this smaller plane that was flying them up to

Swaziland.

Why had she done it? Why? Why? Jean was asking herself. Here she was going to be six thousand miles away from home, going to a strange land to do a job she had never done before and with a man she hardly knew.

They had rarely met during the six weeks. At first it had been to argue about her family. Peter Crosby had said again and again that he wanted them to know. Then to Jean's horror and dismay, she had burst into tears, and Peter had scowled irritably and said if the thought was going to make her hysterical it would be best to forget the family existed! So she had said nothing in her letters until the last one she had written, posting it just before the wedding, in which she had merely said that she had got married and was flying out to Swaziland.

'I'll write and tell you all about it when I get there,' she had, finished, feeling as if a weight had been lifted from her back, for she had dreaded telling them.

The stewardess came down the aisle and gave them coffee and a cake. Peter put down his notes for a short time and glanced at Jean.

'Not scared?' he asked.

'Scared?' she echoed, uncomfortably afraid that he had read her thoughts. Yes, she was scared. Scared to death of this strange man and the strange life that awaited her.

'Scared of flying, I mean,' he said, and a little smile played round his mouth. 'Surely

39

you're not scared of me?'

'No, of course not. I . . .' As usual, Jean thought, she was stumbling over her words. 'I'm just wondering if . . . if . . .'

'You'll do the job? You will. I'll see to that.' Again his voice had changed, a hard note in it. Of course he'd see to it, Jean thought; he was paying her a salary and expected her to earn it!

The coffee drunk, he picked up his notes and she was shut out as if a door had come down between them. She looked at the huge clouds on which they seemed to be floating and at the map-like ground far below with the winding lines of water and the toylike houses.

Maggie had given her a big hug when they said goodbye. 'Best of luck, Jeanie,' she had whispered in Jean's ear, 'but don't expect too much too soon.'

Jean shivered for a moment as she remembered how angry Maggie had been when she returned from Majorca, beautifully sun-browned with plenty of romantic incidents to tell.

'You're *what*?' Maggie had stood in the middle of the room, feet apart, hands on hips, her eyes furious. 'Are you out of your mind? Marrying that man? You must be mad!'

'Sometimes I think I am,' Jean had admitted.

'Then why?' Maggie asked.

It was a question that Jean could never answer however hard she tried. 'I wanted the job—to get away.'

'From your family, of course.' Maggie had understood. that. 'But, Jeannie, we know nothing about him. He might be an alcoholic, a murderer, a con man, a . . . an anything!'

They had both laughed then and Jean had suggested that Maggie should meet Peter. He was agreeable, though he made it plain that it was wasting his time and he could see no reason for it.

It hadn't been a pleasant dinner party, for obviously Maggie did not approve. Not that she mentioned it, of course, for she wasn't supposed to know it was a marriage of convenience. She asked about the children.

'It's tough on them, having to accept two strangers at once. How old are they?' she asked curtly. She had been furious with Jean for not asking earlier.

Peter had startled them both when he admitted that he didn't know.

'But you must know your own nieces and nephews!' Maggie had sounded shocked.

He had smiled. 'I'm afraid I don't. You see, my sister and I grew apart. She married before she was eighteen and I was furious. I disliked him and—well, somehow our paths didn't meet again until just before—before the crash.'

'Yet she made you their guardian? Why not your brother?'

'He's younger than me, married with several

41

children, so I expect she thought he had his hands full. At least, I know their names,' he said with an amused smile.

Much later that evening when they had returned to the flat and were alone Maggie had laid down the law.

'I don't like him, and you're not to marry him,' she said sternly.

'Why don't you like him?' Jean had asked quickly.

And Maggie had frowned. 'I can't put my finger on it . . . define it, so to speak. I have a feeling the whole time that he's taking the mickey out of us, joking, laughing at us. He's very casual about the children.'

'I don't think so,' Jean had returned quickly. 'After all, he could dump them in boarding school. He's making a real sacrifice to look after them.'

'You're impossible, Jeannie! You can't see anything wrong in him—or . . . or you won't. You're young, pretty, your life before you, yet you're going to mess up everything because . . . Maggie had begun, and then, Jean shivered as she remembered, something had seemed to snap inside her and she had almost shouted:

'I know—I'm crazy and a stupid fool. I know I'm doing something I may regret all my life, but . . . but . . . but I love him,' she had wailed, rushing to her bedroom to fling herself on the bed.

Half an hour later Maggie had brought in a

cup of tea and sat on the edge of the bed. She had changed completely.

'You're hoping . . .?' she asked, and when Jean nodded, rubbing the tears from her eyes, Maggie leant forward and kissed her, something she rarely did. 'Good luck,' she had said softly, and had never referred to it again until they said goodbye after the wedding.

The Captain's voice came over the intercom, telling them to do up their safety belts and stop smoking. Peter put away his papers and did up his belt.

'Jean,' he said, 'your belt. What were you dreaming about?'

She looked round. 'I . . . I was thinking of Maggie.'

'Nice girl. Good friend to you,' he said curtly. 'Do up your belt.'

Obeying, she looked out of the window and watched the ground come closer and closer so that she could make out the houses that were so far apart, the forests of trees, the mountains, the red roads winding their way. They circled above the airport, bouncing a little in the clouds, and then Jean closed her eyes as the ground seemed to race up towards them. The plane landed with hardly a bump and finally stopped, everyone undoing their belts, collecting their hand luggage and putting on their coats.

Jean had wondered what to wear for the flight and had been surprised when Peter said

43

it was winter in Swaziland, so wear something warm.

'But it's never cold in Africa . . . the sun always shines,' Jean had said, and Peter laughed.

'A fallacy. My sister has known frost and snow there. It depends where you live. She said they're pretty high up, about four thousand feet above the sea, and it can be cold.'

Now as they walked down the steps to the macadam of the Matsapa airport, Jean was startled by the cold wind that greeted her and was glad she was wearing a silk-lined blue coat over a matching jersey suit. They walked with the other passengers across the macadam to the building where there were people waiting, their faces eager, some with eyes moist with tears as they rushed to greet their relations and friends.

'I arranged for a car to meet us,' Peter told one of the attendants.

A dark-skinned Swazi in a smart khaki jacket and shorts came forward. 'Mr. Crosby?' he asked, and when Peter nodded, the man picked up the luggage and carried it out to the waiting car.

It was a small airport but immaculately tidy, Jean thought, looking round as the car took them down a winding road to what was obviously the main road. Peter Crosby sat silently by her side as the car seemed to fly along the straight road towards the town.

'This must be Manzini,' Peter said as they passed a hospital surrounded by dignified-looking cypresses and past a bus stop where crowds of Swazis were climbing inside the waiting bus. 'We'll have lunch here.'

They stopped outside a hotel—with white steps leading up to a wide verandah that ran round the building. Peter spoke to the driver who was to return in an hour and a half and then his hand was under Jean's elbow as he took her up the stairs. The dining-room was more like a garden with a glass roof and open walls. While Jean studied the menu, Peter went to book a phone call. When he returned, he looked round the half-empty place and then at Jean. 'Well?' he asked. 'Have you decided what you want?'

She felt like saying she wanted to get on a plane that would take her back to England and Maggie's laughter. But it was too late. She had made the decision, now she must stand by it and make the best of it.

'I'm not awfully hungry,' she explained. 'I'm more tired.'

'Didn't you sleep last night?' he asked.

She shook her head and her hair swung forward. 'No,' she said, sweeping it back. 'You did.'

'I was tired. Weren't you?'

'Yes, but . . . well, I couldn't get comfy,' she said. but that was not the truth. She had spent the night thinking of what she had done, wondering how she could be so stupid, wishing she could jump out of the plane. She had little hope that Peter would ever love her, still less since she had seen the picture in the evening paper two nights before—a clear picture of Peter Crosby. 'Well-known Professor of Social Economics, a popular speaker at club dinners, recently touring America successfully and who is often seen with beautiful Charmian Kennet, the famous ballerina.'

The girl had been lovely, out of this world, as Maggie had said, looking over her shoulder.

'Think nothing of it, Jeannie,' Maggie had added. 'What ballerina would want to marry Peter Crosby and be buried alive in a place like Swaziland? I thought he didn't like women.'

'He never said that,' Jean had said quickly. 'Just that he was afraid of marriage.'

But she had thought about it a lot. Charmian Kennet was so beautiful. If Peter had not fallen in love with her he must be anti-woman, even though he would not admit it. It was obvious from the way he talked that his work came first . . . that these books he had been commissioned to write meant more to him than anything else in the world. So her little hope had died almost as soon as it was born.

And now here she was!

She managed a smile. 'I never was good at sleeping in trains either.'

'Well,' he said, 'you can have an early night.

I've booked a phone call to my mother, but it can take hours sometimes, so I think we'll order, as we may have to wait.' He picked up the menu. 'Ah, prawns. What about you?'

'I'd like a grilled sole.'

'Good . . . and we'll have a long cool drink.'

The waiter came and went, and Jean and Peter talked casually about the brilliant purple flowers of a creeper climbing up the trelliswork—the sweet scent of some stocks, the bright colour of the flowers.

'It's hard to think that July is winter,' she commented.

He smiled. 'Yes, everything is turned upside down because we're south of the Equator. But winter will soon be over and spring here. I wonder just how hot it gets in the summer.'

The prawns and sole arrived, and so did a message from the hotel to say the phone call was through.

'Marvellous! My sister wrote that it could take hours,' Peter said as he left her.

Sitting alone, Jean felt as if everyone was staring at her. It made her sensitive and even more clumsy than usual, and by the time Peter returned, she had upset a glass of water, dropped a fork on the floor and lost her napkin.

She looked up and saw he was smiling as he sat down.

'As usual, Mother has acted with discreet diplomacy,' he told her as he began to eat.

'Discreet diplomacy?'

He nodded, his eyes amused. 'She's taken the children away for a week so that we can be alone. Very thoughtful of her.' He chuckled. 'I think I told you she was always pestering me to get married, so her action shows she approves. Not that we need a week alone together, since we're not romanticising, are we?'

Jean looked up and he was staring at her, a smile on his mouth but a strange look in his eyes.

'No . . . no, of course not,' she said quickly, moving her elbow and shooting a knife this time off the table. 'Oh dear!'

Peter laughed. 'It happens to us all. You're tired, which means your reactions are slow.' His face sobered. 'Actually I'm glad Mother did that, because it simplifies things for me.'

'Simplifies?'

He looked surprised. 'Of course. Our sleeping problem. Now I can arrange for separate rooms. If Mother had been there, we would have been faced with a double bed, and if there's one thing I hate, its sleeping on the floor.'

Suddenly Jean was laughing, the kind of laughter that is mixed with tears that mustn't be shed.

'Yes,' she managed to gasp; 'it is a good thing.'

*　　　*　　　*

The drive to the farm seemed endless to Jean. She tried to keep awake in order to look at the beautiful gardens they passed before leaving Manzini and the long straight road that stretched ahead as far as the eyes could see, then they turned on to an earth road. The corrugations shook and jolted the car which went down, down into the valley and then weaved its way up another mountainside. There were few houses, all single-storied, and these now were far apart. Here and there they passed a kraal, as Peter called it, where there were groups of thatched-roof rondavels, which were little round huts outside which the Swazi women would be hoeing their gardens and the small children racing round and a few dogs straying about.

She was aware that Peter was watching her all the time, obviously waiting for her reactions. She decided to attack rather than wait for him to do so.

'Did you think it would be like this?' she asked.

He shrugged. 'Frankly, I didn't think. You see, as I told you, my sister and I rarely corresponded after our quarrel, except for Christmas cards and that sort of thing. Then my mother was ill and my sister wrote to me about her. I was in America at the time. I gathered from Dorothy's letters that she hated Swaziland—I don't know why, but perhaps I shall find out.' His voice was thoughtful.

'Mother found it quite pleasant, but then she plays bridge a lot and Dorothy loathed it. She had quite a chip on her shoulder about that.' Startlingly he smiled at Jean and she felt warm happiness sweep through her for a moment. 'Bill was, apparently, brilliant and nothing poor Dorothy did was ever right, so she gave it up and lost a lot of friends doing that, I gather. Do you play bridge?' In his usual abrupt way, he flung the question at her.

Startled, Jean shook her head. 'I've never tried.'

'Well, we'll have to teach you. It's a useful social quality out here, for there isn't, I gather, much else to do.'

'Look!' Jean pointed to the enormous pile of huge rocks ahead of them. They seemed to be balanced on their pointed ends, climbing up into the blue cloudless sky. The car jostled and shook and suddenly the driver slammed on the brakes as a white goat came sliding down the side of the road. The Swazi turned his head and with a grin apologised.

'The menace of the road, *nkosi*,' he said.

'I can imagine.' Peter leaned forward. 'Do we go through Manbina?'

The Swazi nodded. 'I will tell you, *nkosi*.'

Peter leaned back and smiled. 'Sounds as if the town is so small we shan't recognise it as one!'

Again the car slowed up ; this time a crowd of cattle were strolling down the road, some

50

pausing to turn to give an indignant glare at the car that was disturbing them. Two small boys with strips of bright material tied round their waists came running, shouting, waving the thin sticks in their hands as they tried to get the cattle off the road. Peter thrust his hand in his pocket and tossed some coins to the children and the Swazi, still driving slowly, turned his head and shook it. 'That is bad, *nkosi*. It teaches them to beg.'

'I'm sorry.' Peter sounded as surprised as Jean felt.

The Swazi said, 'Thank you, *nkosi*. You are good, but we want our sons to grow up proud and independent.' He turned back to his job and for a moment Jean and her companion were silent.

Peter gave Jean a shock as he said thoughtfully: 'It seems we have a lot to learn.'

She looked at him. It seemed a strange thing for such a man to admit.

Now the road had come down into a valley and it stretched ahead of them as they drove through forests of pine trees and then past what seemed like hundreds of small trees lined like soldiers on parade.

'Citrus,' Peter said thoughtfully. 'I'd have thought it too hot. I wonder what Bill grew.'

Jean was battling to stay awake. The jolting of the car was like a go-mad rocking chair and she longed to close her eyes and forget the world and the problems that lay ahead of her.

51

The sun was hot, but there was quite a wind blowing the trees about.

'It always seems so odd without hedges or low stone walls,' Peter was saying thoughtfully, and the next thing Jean knew was that she was being gently shaken. She opened her eyes and blinked. Peter was smiling at her, his hand still on her arm.

'Want to see our nearest town?' he asked.

She shook her head, feeling dazed, and then smiled. 'Of course.'

'Our shopping centre,' Peter said sarcastically.

The Swazi had slowed down, as there were notices up as to the speed allowed. They were high on the mountainside, a long winding dangerous-looking road ahead of them.

The Swazi turned. 'We have many accidents here,' he said, almost proudly. 'It is bad, very bad road.'

'The road's all right, depends on the driver,' Peter said quietly as they went down the steep curves and sudden steep inclines. Far below them lay a group of houses. Now as they came closer, there were houses on the way—large single-storied houses, mostly with verandahs round them and gardens ablaze with crimson and purple flowers. Down in the valley they passed a hotel, a two-storied building with a garden in front where there were small tables and brightly coloured sunshades above them.

'The tavern,' the Swazi driver told them.

The car swung round a corner and they were on a straight road with parked cars on either side. There were quite a few people walking along the pavements and there were several stores, a butcher's shop, a greengrocer and two garages.

'This is Manbina,' the driver told them. He turned off down a side street and pointed out a long building surrounded by a cluster of smaller ones. 'The police station,' he said.

They could see several Swazi policemen, walking up and down, immaculately smart in their khaki-coloured uniform. The houses gradually dwindled away and they came to another long building. There was a golf course and a swimming pool where quite a few people were standing, talking.

'The Club,' Peter said thoughtfully. 'It won't see much of me once I've got you launched, but I expect you'll spend a lot of time there. By the way,' again that sudden stare and the crisp voice as he asked a question, 'you can drive a car?'

'Yes.'

'That's a blessing—otherwise I'd have had to teach you. You also said you play golf?'

'Well, not very well,' Jean began, wondering if he was an exceptionally good player.

'You'll soon make friends here,' Peter assured her.

Now they had left behind them the town and the last of the houses, and turned off the road on to an earth track, narrow, with deep ruts as they went slowly through the chaotic mess of rocks and prickly-looking bushes and a few strange trees, their trunks thin and white, their branches bare and sticking out like a witch's angry hand. They went across a thin trickling stream, down the side of it, splashing the water up, and slithering as the car climbed the other side.

'Look!' Jean exclaimed, suddenly excited, and pointed at a monkey who was staring down at them, his eyes bright, but then he was away, swinging from branch to branch. 'A monkey,' she said slowly, sounding more like a child, she realised, than someone capable of looking after three children.

'Obviously your cup of tea,' Peter teased. 'Better any day than a croc, eh?'

Jean laughed, 'I'll learn to cope.'

'I have no doubt,' he told her with a smile, then spoiled it by adding: 'I'll see to that!'

She shivered. For a moment she had forgotten she was just an employee of his, but now again he had reminded her.

The car bumped and slid along the road track through groups of miserable-looking trees, their branches dangling leaflessly.

'That must be Jokosi,' said Peter, his voice shocked.

They had splashed their way through another stream, gone along an avenue of tall trees and round a huge rock at the side of the road. Now they could see they had to climb another mountainside and at the top, also balanced as if copying the habits of the rocks was a house.

The Swazi driver had heard them, for he nodded his head. As the car made its slow way through the bushes and rocks, Jean stared at the house—if it could be called a house. It was a long single-storied building with a tin roof and a verandah. The garden in front had a lawn and a weeping willow and some yellow-flowered trees, whose flowers looked like mimosa. It all looked . . . scruffy, that was the word, she was thinking.

As they came closer, she saw behind it were the farm buildings, large tin sheds in which stood tractors and Swazi moving about, while two Alsatians came racing down the track to greet them, barking loudly.

'You're not allergic to dogs?' Peter asked.

'Of course not.' They were big, lively dogs.

The car drove past the house and round the back, the dogs close behind. As the car stopped, a cat raced across in front and a cock crowed as if in welcome.

Peter had turned to look at Jean and caught her trying in vain to stifle a yawn.

'You're tired,' he said as if surprised.

The Swazi driver opened the car door and as he did so a door of the house opened too. Two Swazi girls came out, in blue cotton dresses and little white aprons. Their black hair was elaborately curled flatly against their heads, their teeth flashed white as they smiled in welcome.

'I am Violet and this is my sister, Dorcas. We speak English.'

'Good,' Peter said briskly.

The Swazi driver was taking the luggage out of the boot and a Swazi boy came running to take it. He was wearing a torn pair of khaki trousers and white shirt.

'That is Solomon,' Violet told them. 'He works in the garden after school.' She led the way indoors while Peter was paying the Swazi driver.

Inside the dark hall, Jean looked around. Her new home! Following Violet, she found herself in a long narrow room that went the width of the building. The furniture was well polished, the silver shining, the windows clean.

'Violet!' Peter called, and Violet hastily vanished. Left alone, Jean went to the window. The verandah outside looked inviting, with canvas chairs and a table. It was very quiet . . . then suddenly the quietness was broken by the shrill crowing of a cock and the roar of an engine somewhere.

Jean wondered what to do. Look for Peter? But he had called Violet, not her! She sat down in one of the chairs, stretched out her long legs and yawned—a long, satisfying yawn as she leant back against the high inviting back of the chair and closed her eyes. At least they were here, she thought sleepily. This room looked nice at any rate and the chair was beautifully com . . .

The sound of voices woke her and she sat up, suddenly aware that she must look a mess as Peter came into the room with a short man by his side, a man with sun-tanned skin, blond hair and a surprised expression as he looked at her.

'My poor little wife is tired,' Peter was saying, his voice amused. Jean, half-asleep, blinked her eyes. So Peter was married, she began to think, and her thoughts jerked to a standstill. Of course Peter had a wife—*she* was his poor little wife!

'Jean, I want you to meet Luke Whitwell, the manager. Whitwell, this is my wife,' Peter said, his voice still amused as if he had made a joke that no one else recognised.

Jean struggled to her feet, her hand clasped in the stranger's for a moment, and he smiled.

'Nice to see you, Mrs. Crosby. I hope you'll be happier here than . . .' He stopped speaking abruptly and looked worried.

Peter smiled. 'I know, Whitwell. My sister wasn't happy here, was she?'

'It's a small community and she was bored,' Luke Whitwell shrugged. 'This is a place you either love or hate.'

'We intend to love it, don't we, Jean?' said Peter, his arm going lightly round her shoulder.

Startled at the affection in his voice, Jean stared up at him. She saw the laughter in his eyes and it was like a candle being blown out—the momentary happiness was wiped away. Of course, she had forgotten that Peter had said that, in front of other people, they would pretend it was a real marriage, not a phoney one!

She managed a smile. 'I'm sure we shall . . .' she began, but was stopped by the biggest yawn she had ever given. 'I'm sorry, but . . .'

'I know,' Peter said with a smile. 'You're not used to flying, Jean, and it can be very exhausting, surprisingly so. An early night.'

Luke Whitwell turned away. 'I'll see you morrow, then, Mr. Crosby?'

'Yes. I'll be leaving everything to you, of course, but I would like to get a picture of what's going on.'

'Not very well, I'm afraid.' The blond-haired man looked concerned. 'We need money here. The trouble we have with our old tractors, the time we waste!'

'We'll discuss that tomorrow,' Peter told him, and almost hustled him out, Jean thought, as she stretched her arms, ran her hand through her mass of dark hair and yawned again. The manager seemed quite nice, friendly, though his surprise was plain. Surely he had known? Peter's mother would have told him that Peter had got married?

Peter came back. 'Everything's under

control,' he said cheerfully but with a definitely impersonal tone. 'This way.' He led her down a long corridor that ran the length of the single-storied house, opened the door of a large room with a huge double bed in it. 'I'll give that to my mother,' he said.

'Is she . . . will she live with us?' Jean asked, startled and a little worried.

Laughing, Peter shook his head. 'Not on your life, but she'll want to stay for a few days. It wouldn't work, Jean. I'm fond of her and she says she loves me dearly, but everything I do irritates her and everything she does irritates me. We get on well if we don't meet too often.' He closed the door and walked on, opening another door.

'This is your room,' he said. 'The girls have made the bed. It's one of the guest rooms, I gather. Seems like my sister entertained a lot.'

Jean walked into the room. It was large, but there was a big window giving her a clear view of the valley below. The palm trees lined a wide set of steps that obviously led down to the valley. On the left she could see the farm buildings, huge sheds with tin roofs, dogs running round, a tractor surrounded by Swazis who were laughing and talking. She yawned again, half asleep, noticing vaguely that the curtains were pale blue, that the floor was highly polished and a rug by the single bed. There were built-in cupboards and a small dressing-table and that was all.

'I'm afraid it's not very luxurious,' Peter said, his voice amused, 'but . . .'

'It's . . .' Jean yawned. 'It's fine.'

He went to the door, turned and smiled at her. 'I'm sleeping in the room opposite. There's a key in your door if you don't trust me.'

She felt herself blushing. 'Of course I trust you!'

Staring at her, his eyes narrowed, Peter gave a little unamused laugh. 'I wonder if you should. After all, I am a man.'

He left the room, and as he closed the door, Jean put her hands to her face. How could she have been so stupid, so crazy? she asked herself. She hadn't a hope of making him love her; it all amused him. How was she to bear the years ahead? Living in the same house with a man you love and who merely sees you as someone useful.

The door opened and she jumped, wondering who it was as she lowered her hands. It was Peter again.

He smiled. 'I forgot to say good-night. Don't bother to join me for dinner. Go to bed and Violet will bring you something to eat. See you in the morning.'

'Good . . . good-night,' Jean managed to say, then stared at the door that was slowly closing.

She lay down on the bed, her hair falling over her face, getting entangled as her tears came. She was a fool, an utter fool. How was she going to bear it all? How?

CHAPTER THREE

During the next few days Jean often felt like Alice in *Alice in Wonderland*, drifting through a strange unknown world, sometimes happy, sometimes sad. It was so completely different a life from the one she knew that she had to adjust, and she often found herself understanding why Peter's sister had been so unhappy. Maybe it would be better when the children came, she would think. Not that *all* the day was sad—it was only the part of the day when Peter vanished and she was alone.

Her first night had set the pattern: if she could not be of use, then he didn't want to see her.

She had slept like a log, awakened by Violet bringing her a tray of roast chicken, followed by a chocolate mousse. Then Jean had wearily unpacked, undressed, and gone to bed to sleep soundly, only to be awakened hours later when she heard loud voices shouting and laughing. The sun was pouring in through the window, so she leapt out of bed and hurried to see where the sounds came from.

Looking sideways she could see the farm buildings and there was a long truck into which the Swazis of both sexes were climbing, laughing, shouting, some singing. Glancing at her watch, Jean saw it was six a.m., so she hurried back to bed, to be awakened by Violet with breakfast on a tray.

Never in her life had Jean known such treatment. It was lovely to be spoiled, she had thought, yet as the days passed, she found it irritating, for there was nothing at all for her to do. And how could you do nothing at all *all* the time? This, she realised, was her problem and one she had to solve. But how?

The first day she had bathed, carefully chosen a pale yellow cotton dress and wandered through the quiet house, for there seemed no one in it. She found the room where obviously two boys slept. She looked curiously at the books and comics, and wondered what their ages were. Not very young, she thought, but not very old. Further along the corridor, she found the girl's room. On the wall were plastered pin-up pictures of well-known pop singers and her dressing-table was covered with different cosmetics as if she was experimenting.

The kitchen, large, airy and clean, was empty. Where was everyone? Jean wondered. She found a half open door and could see a desk inside. Was this going to be Peter's? She hesitated outside, but when the silence made her certain he was not there, she looked in. It was a small room with a large window, the desk and chair, and bookshelves. But no Peter.

So she went outside on to the verandah—which later she was to learn was called a *stoep*—and dozed in the sunshine until lunch when Peter arrived with the farm manager.

But, as the days passed, she felt more and more as if she was on another planet, or had landed on the moon. There was nothing at all to do! You couldn't sit for ever in the sunshine, dozing, listening with amusement to Violet and Dorcas chattering and laughing as they worked together. Out on the clothes line, the washing would flap in the wind, and as it dried, Dorcas would iron the clothes. After two days of breakfast in bed and no sign of Peter, Jean got up early so that they had breakfast together.

No newspaper, either, that was another strange thing, and Peter agreed that he missed it.

'You can always get a copy in Manbina, I'm told, but it will be two days old.'

Then Peter would vanish into his study and she would not see him until lunch time. Again he would vanish and not appear again until about five o'clock, when he would take her down to the Club or the hotel for a drink before dinner or sometimes have the meal there.

This was the happiest part of the day for Jean. It was not due to meeting new people, for this had always embarrassed her and she seemed to act even more clumsily than ever when Peter introduced her to Dorothy's friends. They in turn introduced the newly-married couple to other friends so that Jean's mind became a muddled, chaotic mess as she tried to remember their names. No, she enjoyed the evenings because Peter was with her. Often his affectionate manner made her forget that he was only acting the part of a loving husband. As he had said, they must act the part of a happy couple, and there were times when she had turned to him impulsively and then had wondered if she had shown him the truth—that she was not acting at all!

Gradually, through talking to her new friends, Jean learned more about Dorothy and the children. The eldest child was called Vanessa, a girl of thirteen.

'You'd think she was four years older,' one woman told her. 'Precocious.' Hugh was ten, 'A quiet boy, as if he has retreated from reality,' Jean was told. Nick, it seemed, was the favourite. 'A brilliant brain,' 'Friendly little lad,' 'His mother's favourite—he must be finding it hardest,' was said. 'Spoilt brat,' said another woman.

Jean also learned of Dorothy's unhappiness.

'She couldn't adjust to this life. She wouldn't play bowls or bridge or mix. I hope you'll be different,' one of Jean's new friends said.

At their suggestion Jean joined the library and took home a pile of books one evening. Peter, driving slowly through the wildness, looked down at her.

'Tomorrow we'll go for a drive—only you'll

drive,' he told her.

The car was a big one, and Jean frowned as she looked at the gears, very different from her father's.

'Okay?' he asked. 'It'll make you independent. You can drive into town and go to the coffee parties.'

'The children?' she began.

'You'll have to drive them into school each morning and bring them back, so you might as well stay in there,' Peter pointed out.

Jean looked at the tall man by her side. He was frowning as he drove, watching for the goats that could appear without warning. He wanted her out of the way. Did it annoy him even to know she was in the house while he worked, although she never made any attempt to interrupt him?

'And when it rains?'

His face relaxed into a smile. 'Not to worry. The tractor can come along and rescue you. By the way, how do you like Luke?'

Once again, he was throwing a question at her without any warning.

'Luke? He's . . . well, I quite like him,' Jean said, and it was true. Luke often came in when Peter was at work and the two of them would sit in the sunshine and talk—talk of Cornwall where he was born, talk of his parents emigrating and finally coming to Swaziland.

'I love it here,' Luke had said simply. 'I never want to leave it.'

Now Peter nodded. 'Yes, so do I. He's been doing a difficult job here. Maybe things will be easier now that more money is available.'

'It is? I thought you said . . .'

Peter, deftly evading a slow-going goat, smiled. 'Yes, things were bad, but they'll be all right now.'

'You mean you . .?' Somehow she had never thought about Peter having money or not.

'Yes. I had a grandfather who left me some and I was wisely advised as to my investments. Dorothy had the same, but unfortunately not the good advice I got.'

'But you're not a farmer. Wouldn't it be better to sell the farm?'

Peter shrugged. 'I suppose I could, but somehow I think it would be better for the children if I stay on so that I can hand it over when they're old enough to cope with it.'

'But do either of the boys want to farm?'

'According to Luke, Hugh might. He, it seems, is a loner, and a farmer's life, especially out here, is pretty lonely. You have to be able to live alone to stick it. I don't think I could live here for ever. It's ideal for my present work, but . . . '

But—what a strange word that was, Jean was thinking as the farm came into view. *But* can mean so much. She was happy here, *but* only when Peter was with her. Peter was happy here, *but* only when he was working on his books. A little word, but one that can make all the difference in the world.

The next day she drove the car. With Peter by her side, she felt nervous and was, of course, clumsy and stupid. After several bad mistakes she turned to him impulsively.

'I thought I could drive!' she sighed.

He smiled. 'You will be able to—everything here is so different.'

'Oh, it is . . . so very different. I hate to think of driving in heavy rain They say the mud is so thick and slippery.'

Peter put his hand over hers, the first affectionate movement he had ever made when they were alone.

'Not to worry,' he said. 'I'll cope with that until you get used to it. Now, we'll start again. Just forget I'm here. I'll shut my eyes and leave it all to you.' He leaned back, folded his arms and closed his eyes.

It was difficult driving with these deep ruts, and unexpected stones and sharp turns and sudden steep drops down into a valley. But, as the morning passed, so did Jean's fear of looking stupid go. She grew more confident and even enjoyed the drive back, having mastered the art of gear-changing and goats.

There was a car parked outside the house, and Peter frowned. 'They're back early,' he commented.

'Is it your mother?' Jean asked, suddenly nervous again. If only she wasn't so tall and clumsy! How could she make a good impression?

As they got out of the car, the front door of the house opened. A small, slight, white-haired woman stood there, wearing a bright yellow dress, a smile on her slightly wrinkled face.

'Peter, my dear boy! And this is your wife.' She turned to Jean and her whole face changed, going very white, her eyes startled. 'You're his wife?' Mrs. Crosby said very slowly as Jean walked towards her.

'Yes.' Peter spoke quickly. 'This is Jean, my wife. Jean—my mother.'

'But I . . . but . . .' Mrs. Crosby stumbled over her words and then obviously made a great effort to pull herself together. 'How nice to meet you, Jean,' she said, holding out her hand. The words were welcoming, the voice was not. Jean wondered why.

'How are the children?' Peter asked.

'I left them with Leila Tamson. I thought I'd like to see you and . . . and . . .' Colour filled the old lady's white cheeks. 'Your wife,' she added. 'Leila is bringing them out later and I've asked her to stay for dinner. You have met Leila?' she asked Jean.

'I don't think so,' Jean said slowly. 'I'm afraid I'm not good at remembering names.'

'What a pity. It can be so awkward,' said Mrs. Crosby.

Jean glanced at Peter and saw that his face was completely relaxed, his eyes twinkling, and his mouth had that triumphant smile she

68

was growing to know so well. He had achieved something. But what could it be?

'No, you haven't a good memory, Jean,' he said, his arm going round her shoulders. 'But you have met a lot. We've been to the Club and the hotel, Mother, but we haven't met the Tamsons. I've heard of them.'

'They're a nice couple. Dorothy was very fond of them. They don't drink,' Mrs. Crosby added. 'Well, come in, come in. Lunch is ready. Where have you been?'

'Jean was practising her driving. We should have met you, but we turned off down the main road away from Manbina.'

They went inside. Mrs. Crosby had obviously something to say to Peter, but she didn't want to say it in front of his wife, Jean realised, so she murmured an excuse, and as she hurried down the corridor, just heard a few words from her mother-in-law's shrill voice sounding accusing. 'I got it all ready.'

Jean heard no more. She hurried to her room, wondering how Peter was explaining the separate rooms in which they were sleeping, especially as this was supposed to be their honeymoon.

When the gong boomed, Jean hurried to join the others, a little worried as to how Mrs. Crosby had accepted Peter's explanation, but she was surprised at the warmth of Mrs. Crosby's greeting. Whatever Peter had said, his mother had not only accepted it but it had made her more friendly to her new, unknown daughter-in-law.

Luke joined them for lunch, at Mrs. Crosby's suggestion, and the meal went easily, conversation never faltering. Afterwards Peter and Luke vanished and Jean was left alone with his mother. They sat in the long lounge. Mrs. Crosby didn't like the sunshine. 'Too many cases of skin cancer out here for my liking,' she said. 'I was always on at my daughter about it.'

Jean looked round her rather wildly, feeling she was trapped. She should have picked flowers and arranged them in this room, but she had not thought of it. As if Mrs. Crosby could read Jean's thoughts, she went on:

'You've a lot to learn, my dear. Running a home isn't easy, nor is bringing up children. Dorothy was a good mother, a very good mother indeed, but she's spoilt Nicky. You must be more strict with him—he takes advantage.'

Jean murmured answers, grateful to have Mrs. Crosby talk about the children. She was wishing she could have spoken to Peter before this . . . this kind of inquisition, for that was how she felt, dreading the questions Mrs. Crosby might ask because the wrong answers could be easily given. Surely Peter could have seen that?

'You haven't known Peter long?' Mrs. Crosby asked abruptly. Jean was speechless for a moment. Peter's mother had his disconcerting habit of asking questions without warning.

'Long enough,' she said, trying to smile.

Mrs. Crosby looked worried. 'I wonder. Peter isn't an easy man to live with.'

You're telling me. Jean felt like saying, but merely nodded.

'He's in love with his work,' Mrs. Crosby went on. 'You'll lead a lonely life.'

'I know. He warned me.'

'I wonder if you realise just how lonely. Dorothy hated it here, hated every moment she was here.'

'I think I'll . .' Jean began.

'You think! I wonder if you thought long enough before you married Peter. He's much older than you, obviously you don't share many interests except . . .' Mrs. Crosby gave a funny little grunt, 'except drinking. What made you marry him, Jean?'

Jean's mouth was suddenly dry. Just what had Peter told his mother? Yet if he had told her the truth, surely he would have warned his pseudo-wife?

'I love him,' she said.

'You really love him?' Mrs. Crosby said slowly. 'But how can you know you love anyone when you've only known them for so short a time?'

'I . . . I knew the very first time I saw him,' Jean faltered.

'Love at first sight!' Mrs. Crosby grunted again. 'How romantic! Well, it seems Cupid shot very accurately, because that's exactly what Peter said.'

'He said . . . that?' Jean almost whispered, and then her momentary happiness vanished. Of course he would—the perfect actor, and lying when acting is not lying.

A car came up the hill and Jean was glad, for she was afraid of any more questions. They both stood up and looked out of the window— just as Peter joined them.

'Is that the children?' he asked.

He opened the window and as they watched, a short plump woman in a pale blue trouser suit, her fair hair in short curls round her head, got out of the driver's seat. At the same time the doors of the back of the car opened and a thin boy with dark hair got out. He saw them waiting and came rushing towards them, shouting: 'Nana . . . Nana . . . here we are!'

Another boy, a few years older, also got out. He was quite different, with longish fair hair, and his blue eyes were wary Jean saw as he came towards the house. Last of all came a girl—tall, slender, wearing a psychedelic-coloured dress, its stripes in different shades of green that seemed to make her reddish hair look almost golden in the sunlight.

She came quickly, staring beyond them. 'Where is she?' she asked eagerly.

Mrs. Crosby looked pale. 'Children, this is

your Uncle Peter and your Auntie Jean.'

Jean was conscious that they were all staring at her as if puzzled, then Vanessa spoke, her green eyes flashing with anger. 'She can't be! She's too tall. Nana, you said the was a ballerina . . .'

There was a sudden hush. Jean glanced from one face to another and finally at Peter's. He wasn't looking annoyed, only amused. Suddenly Jean understood—everything: Mrs. Crosby's surprise when Peter produced his bride, Luke's and now Vanessa's. Peter had let them believe he was going to marry Charmian Kennet, the world-famous ballerina and the beautiful girl Jean had seen him with in the photograph in the evening paper just before the wedding.

CHAPTER FOUR

Jean's hope that having the children to look after might make her life more endurable was soon destroyed. Perhaps the destruction began when they all met, for never, ever, would she forget the silence that followed Vanessa's angry cry: 'She's much too tall! You told me she was a ballerina!'

Peter's sudden burst of laughter had broken the stillness and brought Jean out of her dazed state.

'You must have been joking, Mother. I've known Charmian for years, but there's never been any question of marriage. She's too wrapped up in her future to waste time in marriage,' he added scornfully.

His mother looked uncomfortable. 'Somehow I thought . . . it's often in the papers that you were seen . . . '

'With her? Sure I was. And with a hundred other beautiful girls, but that doesn't mean I intended to marry any of them. You're always thinking things, Mother,' he added, this time his voice was tender. Then his arm had gone round Jean's shoulders as he he pulled her close so that their bodies were touching. 'This is the girl I married.' He bent and kissed her cheek gently.

Jean caught her breath with dismay, for she was filled with the desire to turn towards him, linking her arms round his neck, lifting her mouth to his. It was a strange feeling—one she had never felt before in her life, and one she must control, for it was something she must not do, because he would immediately know the truth. Something he must never find out.

Somehow she managed to smile. 'I'm sorry you're disappointed,' she said to Vanessa, who was glaring at her.

'Vanessa's a good dancer. She goes to special classes,' Mrs. Crosby said proudly.

'Well, welcome to Manbina,' a slight husky voice interrupted, and Peter looked round.

The short plump, fair-haired woman who had brought the children was smiling, and again Mrs. Crosby looked upset.

'Oh, dear, how very rude of me! Leila dear, please forgive me. This is Peter, my son; and . . . and Jean, my daughter-in-law. Peter . . . I mean, Jean, because of course you come first.' Mrs. Crosby's laughter was unsteady. 'This is Leila Tamson, a good friend of ours.' She turned to the children. 'Indoors, all of you,' she ordered, and led the way.

Lelia Tamson was smiling. Her eyes were friendly, Jean thought. 'I do hope you're happier here than poor Dorothy was,' Leila said as they followed the children inside. 'Though it was really her fault, poor darling. I mean, liking or hating a place so often depends on your own character, doesn't it?' She laughed, her voice warm. 'I expect you've heard of that old quotation: "Love converts the hut into a palace of gold"?' She turned to smile at them. 'This isn't much of a palace, but I expect it will be to you two!'

Before Jean could speak, Peter had answered. 'I'm sure it will, won't it, darling?' he asked, smiling down at her.

Jean had no idea that her eyes were filled with startled fear as she looked up at him, nor that he could plainly see that she didn't know how to answer, so he laughed again: 'You are staying to dinner, Mrs. Tamson? Where's your husband?'

'Can't you guess?' Leila laughed. 'Down at the Club. Ted practically lives there. Most men do. I haven't been down lately as I've had my mother staying with me, but now she's flown back to England and I'm alone in the evenings. I'll probably go, too.' She smiled at Jean. 'One gets most awfully bored, you know. The women at one end of the bar, the men at the other. What is there to talk about: Our children —trouble with the servants, and,' she laughed, 'gossip! I often wonder how we'd survive without that.'

'Exactly,' Peter agreed, his voice strange. 'I gathered that from my sister. I told you, didn't I, Jean?'

Jean had found her voice by now. 'Yes. I know already how right you were,' she added, and glancing up at him saw by the look in his eyes that he understood what she meant. Already in this short time she had been amazed at what she had heard. Now she could imagine what the local grapevine would have made of Peter and his young governess!

'Never mind,' Leila said with a smile. 'I'm sure you'll be happy here, my dear. I know I am, though at first I wondered how I'd ever stand it. When I married Ted, he had a job in London and we had a charming house at Weybridge, then we came out to this.' She waved her hand vaguely. 'You can imagine how different it was!'

Later in the evening, after Leila—as she

76

insisted on being called—had left and Peter's mother, pleading a headache, had left them and the children were all in bed, or in their own rooms, Jean asked Peter outright if he had deliberately encouraged his mother to think he was going to marry Charmian Kennet.

'You looked pleased as anything,' she said accusingly. 'And it was most embarrassing for me.'

He smiled. 'Sorry. No, I'd no idea Mother was thinking that, although I should have guessed it from what she said on the phone about hoping you wouldn't miss your glamorous life.'

Jean felt her mouth quivering into a smile. 'It certainly didn't apply to me!'

'Precisely,' Peter laughed. 'Mother is a romanticist, always adding two and two together, hoping or dreaming it makes six. As for Charmian, she's the last person I'd want to live with—temperamental, egotistical, dedicated to her own work, intent on a famous future, hardly good qualities for a wife.' He looked at his watch. 'Good, we're quite early tonight. I can get some work done. Goodnight.' He turned away and went towards his small study.

As they walked down the corridor, a blare of music seemed to burst through the door of Vanessa's room. Peter frowned.

'Tell her to tone it down, Jean. I can't work with that noise.'

'Me tell her?' Jean began, her eyes wide with dismay.

He frowned. 'Yes. Isn't that why you're here?' he asked. 'To keep the kids out of my way?'

It hurt, though it was the truth. He was right—this was what he was paying her for!

She knocked on Vanessa's door. 'Who's there?' the girl's shrill voice asked.

'. . . Er . . . Aunt Jean,' Jean managed to say.

'What do you want?' Vanessa shouted.

'To speak to you.'

'Come in, then. Door isn't locked,' Vanessa told her, so Jean obeyed, opened the door and went in.

The room was vibrating with the sound of music. Vanessa was sprawled on the bed in a pair of mini-pyjamas, her reddish hair twisted round into a bun on top of her head, her face beautiful with high cheekbones and a pointed chin.

'So what?' she said rudely.

'Uncle Peter has to work now, so he would like the music softer,' Jean said quietly.

Vanessa pulled a face. 'What's the good? It's not music when it's quiet. I like it loud.'

'So do I,' Jean said.

'You do?' Vanessa sat up, startled. 'Then why . . .'

'Because your uncle has been commissioned to write these books and it means a lot of work. He's gone now to his study to write and

78

he can't do it with the music so loud. Look,' Jean said with a smile, 'suppose tomorrow we find somewhere in the garden and get a sort of summerhouse built where we can play as loud as we like?'

Vanessa nodded slowly. 'That's an idea,' she said, putting out her arm, stretching it till her hand reached the small transistor and she switched it off. She looked up at Jean. 'I wish you were a ballet dancer. You could have helped me.'

'I'm sorry,' Jean smiled. 'When I was young, I wanted to be one too.'

'Then why weren't you?'

'Isn't it obvious?' Jean shrugged her shoulders. 'You said it when you saw me—"she's too tall." That was it. I was a giant compared with the others.'

'Do you mind? Not dancing, I mean.'

'I did, at first. It was sort of a dream, you see. I was to be beautiful, famous, a wonderful dancer with the most famous partners,' Jean laughed. 'Then as I grew older, I realised I wasn't beautiful.'

Vanessa frowned. 'You could be, you know. You've got one of those high foreheads. Why don't you sweep your hair back from your face?'

'You think so?' Jean was surprised, because it was just what Peter had said.

'Look.' Vanessa slid off the bed and went to her wardrobe. 'I've got a wig,' she said

79

proudly. 'Have you?' She produced a platinum blonde wig, stood by the mirror, putting it on, adjusting it with a little frown, then swinging to look at Jean, 'Well, what do you think?'

It was all Jean could do not to laugh. 'It makes you look years older.'

'Good!' Vanessa clapped her hands. 'I want to look older, because I like older men. I've got no time for boys of my age—so immature and stupid. They don't know what to talk about.' She frowned. 'I hope Uncle Peter isn't going to be like Dad was.'

Jean had turned away, her hand on the door handle. Now she looked round. 'How do you mean?'

'He was frightfully square. Said I was too young to go to dances. That's ridiculous, isn't it? I mean, I'm nearly fourteen and . . .' Vanessa smiled suddenly. 'Didn't you go dancing when you were my age?'

Jean shook her head. 'My parents were very strict, too.'

'Good.' Vanessa looked pleased. 'Then you'll be on my side,' she said triumphantly.

Murmuring good-night. Jean escaped quickly. That was a question she couldn't answer. How could she be on Vanessa's side when Peter was paying her to look after the girl? In any case, thirteen was rather young.

In her bedroom, Jean gazed close in the mirror. She had been Vanessa's age only nine years or so ago. How had she felt? Had she

80

resented her parents' strictness, had she felt badly treated? Her face relaxed in a smile, for she had! Yet now, years later, she could see the other side of it. The reasons her parents had been like that, simply because they loved her.

She frowned. That was odd—for never once before had she thought that they did love her. Yet now she could understand that their strictness was because of love and concern for her. They were so afraid of drugs, the thought of their daughter being an unmarried mother, and she could remember almost screaming at them that she was no fool and could take care of herself! Yet today she saw everything differently. Perhaps it would help her handle Vanessa. She hoped so, because she could see Vanessa was going to be awkward as so many girls of her age were.

'Including myself,' she told the reflection she gazed at. Suddenly she lifted her hair, twisted it on top of her head and looked at her face, no longer half hidden by the dark hair that fell forward but showed her high forehead and cheekbones. Maybe she would try her hair like that. She had been told of someone in Manbina who did hairdressing in her own home.

She went to bed and fell asleep at once.

In the morning, Peter drove with her and the children to the school. This was down in a valley, some fifteen miles away. It was near a hotel and two large rival stores. Vanessa hardly talked, she was reading a magazine. The boys were squabbling, and Peter turned to frown at them.

'You can fight where you like,' he said, 'but not in my car.'

'It isn't your car,' Nick said. 'It's Dad's.'

Peter laughed. 'You're right, it was, but it's mine now.'

When the children had left them, Peter turned to look at Jean thoughtfully.

'Well? How are things going? I notice Vanessa did what she was told last night. Surprised me. Did you twist her arm?' he smiled.

'No. I explained that you had to work. Peter, could we build a small music room in the garden, a sort of summerhouse. I mean, when you're Vanessa's age, music isn't music unless it's blindingly noisy. I used to feel the same.'

'And of course as you're only a few years older than she is,' he said drily, 'it helps you understand.'

'It's funny,' Jean was twisting her fingers together, frowning a little as they sat there, watching the children leap from cars, scurrying into the school. 'It's as if I'm in two worlds,' she said slowly. 'I can understand Vanessa's point of view—but I can see ours, too.'

'Ours?' he queried.

'Yes. Well, we are in a way her parents.'

'I see, or I think I do. You're beginning to

see the parents' side of the question.'

Jean looked up at him, her face puzzled. 'Yes, I am. It's odd in a way.'

'I don't think so,' said Peter, his voice suddenly curt as he started the engine. 'It merely means you're growing up at last.' He drove down towards the stores. 'You can do some shopping here after bringing the kids to school. There's a library here, too, two days a week, but you'll be told all that. You needn't come back if you don't want to, because the children come out at one o'clock. Vanessa has homework she must do. That's up to you, of course,' he said as he drove rapidly down the long straight road, his voice changing, becoming curt and impersonal.

Mrs. Crosby was sitting on the *stoep* and Jean joined her for a cup of coffee. Peter, of course, disappeared into his study.

'Well?' the older woman asked, her eyes sympathetic. 'I know you'll do your best, my dear, but I warn you, Peter can be very difficult.'

'The understatement of the year,' Jean said, laughing a little. 'Actually it's the children that worry me. I'm not used to coping with them, and Vanessa . . . '

'Is going through that difficult stage of not being old enough or young enough. You may find Hugh equally difficult, only in a different way. He retreats from the world and stares at you out of uninterested eyes. I don't know

83

how to explain them, but it's as if he doesn't see you. He rarely talks except to Nick. I think he felt the shock of the tragedy the most. He loved his mother—too much, I'm afraid, for she had time only for Nick. That lad's been sadly spoilt by us all, so you may get trouble there. I do hope you'll manage all right.' Mrs. Crosby sighed. 'It won't be easy for any of you.'

She left them a few days later, pleading a terrible lethargy that made the slightest act an ordeal. Jean thought the truth was that it was because Peter had lost his temper twice with Nick for being cheeky and although Mrs. Crosby agreed that the boy deserved to be punished, at the same time she had obviously wanted to defend him. It hadn't been an easy few days, Jean thought, as she watched Peter drive his mother away. She was going to the airport and flying to Durban where she would stay for a few weeks before deciding what to do in the future.

The children had been given a lift to school by Leila who would also bring them back, so Jean found herself alone. Not really, for she could hear Violet and Dorcas both laughing and talking loudly as they cleaned the house.

Jean looked round. It was a beautiful view, there was no doubt. The garden she loved with its gay bushes and dramatic-looking purple flowers on the arches, and the stone steps that went down towards the river and that she had never been down yet. The sun was warm but not hot. It was still a kind of spring, though Africa had no real division between winter and summer. Sometimes the evenings were cold; if they stayed at home, there would be a blazing log fire that enticed you to sit close to it. Most evenings Peter would be taking her to the Club or the hotel for a drink before dinner, being the perfect husband, making sure she had companions with whom to talk, a drink in her hand, and looking happy. Jean always felt happy at these times, for she could pretend, and succeed in fooling herself, that that was how he felt . . . a fantasy that was soon destroyed, for as they reached the farmhouse Peter would change, become impersonal, even indifferent, hastily eating dinner and vanishing into his study so she would have lonely evenings to spend now that Mrs. Crosby had gone.

With the long morning stretching ahead, Jean decided to write to her parents. She had not heard from them since she wrote to say she was getting married and it was only that morning that she had realised something— something that made her feel ashamed, for it had been a terrible thing to do. She had written to say she was going to live in Swaziland, but at no time had she given them her address.

How could she have forgotten? she wondered. Now, as she began to write to them, she felt horribly guilty. If she had a daughter who had got married, merely telling her so at the last moment, not bothering to write, not even bothering to give her address—how would she have felt? she wondered. Either hurt or furiously angry, she decided.

'I'm terribly sorry I haven't written before, but everything seems to have happened at once and although I have all the time in the world, yet I never seem to have time for anything We were married in a hurry and Peter had to fly out immediately. He has been commissioned to write a number of books and works all day long. His two nephews and a niece live with us. The scenery is fantastic, the most gorgeous mountains and gardens filled with purple and red or yellow flowers, really lovely. I've made a lot of friends already, and although it sounds lonely, actually it isn't as lonely as it was in London. I'll get some photos taken and let you have them so that you can see how very beautiful it is here,' she wrote, going on to explain about the distances and how no one bothered if it was a hundred miles to go to what they called a bioscope or to watch a match or visit a friend. She told them about the white egrets who were always round the horses and cows, waiting for the hooves to disturb the ground so that they could find the worms. She wrote about the honey birds, and the strange one who sounded a little like a cuckoo, but she didn't mention the crocodiles. Indeed, she realised as she finished the letter, she had heard nothing about them. Had Peter been teasing when he talked about them?

She read the letter, amazed at the length and the ease with which it had been written—perhaps because for the first time she had written as she felt.

Peter returned later, looking tired. Jean and the children were playing in the garden, Jean watching the beauty of the sun as slowly and with a dignity of its own it dropped down behind the mountains, the sky being a wonderful mixture of yellows and red.

'Uncle Peter,' Nick asked him as Peter joined them, 'Uncle Ted and Aunt Leila sleep together in a big bed—why don't you and Aunt Jean do the same?'

There was a sudden silence. Jean looked across the children's heads at Peter, wondering how he would react. Would he call it cheeky?

But Peter was laughing, looking over his shoulder, lifting his finger to his mouth. 'This is a secret, Nicky boy. You mustn't tell anyone or they'll laugh at poor Auntie Jean.' He glanced up at her, his eyes amused. 'I may tell them?' he asked, and didn't wait for an answer but went on, 'You see, Auntie Jean walks in her sleep.'

'She does?' Nick's eyes were wide open. 'Why?'

'We don't know why. She walks very quietly and I have the room opposite her so that if I hear the door open, I wake up and can go and stop her and take her back to her bed without even waking her up.'

'She doesn't know?' Nick frowned.

'No. She never wakes up. If I woke her up, she might fall over and hurt herself. You see?'

Nick nodded his head solemnly. 'She doesn't know,' he said, his voice sad.

'No. So it's no good asking her, because she doesn't believe me when I tell her, but if ever you see her wandering round in the middle of the night, don't ever wake her but come to me. Right?'

'Right,' Nick agreed, nodding again.

Vanessa was looking puzzled. She turned to Jean.

'Have you always walked in your sleep?'

Again before Jean could speak, Peter stepped in. 'As I told you, she doesn't know it. You see, we never wake her up, so she knows nothing about it.'

The gong sounded and they all turned to go indoors, the children racing ahead. Peter walked by Jean's side, his arm lightly round her shoulder. He looked down at her startled face.

'Well?' he asked.

'Do I really walk in my sleep?' she asked him quietly, turning to stare at him worriedly.

He smiled. 'Of course not. Would you have preferred me to tell them the truth?'

CHAPTER FIVE

As the days passed, becoming weeks—each one with a different problem to face—Jean found herself slipping into place, adjusting herself to this new and utterly strange life.

Her day started at seven when Dorcas brought her a cup of tea; Jean would then shower and dress and hurry to the kitchen to tell Dorcas what they would have for lunch and then join the children at breakfast before driving them down to school. Unused as she was to catering for five people, it wasn't always easy. Peter declared himself indifferent to food but liked plenty of protein. The children were easier, all shouting loudly the kind of food they liked. Jean did her best to satisfy them all, but what worried her most was the cost. True, having a deep-freeze meant she could buy meat in bulk and much cheaper. Shopping at the big stores was simplicity itself, going round, choosing what she wanted, and an assistant carried the huge cardboard box outside to tuck it away in the boot of the car. Having accounts meant she actually spent little money in cash, but when the bills came with the goods, she often got worried, for Peter had said nothing about how much money she might spend. He never said anything, but she was always alert in case he would have a change of mood and suddenly accuse her of being carelessly extravagant.

Peter was not an easy man to live with, just as his mother had said. He was angry with the children if they made too much noise—he frowned disapprovingly at Vanessa's clothes. In fact he was, as Vanessa said, very square at times. Yet other days he would chat to the children, making them laugh as he described some of his adventures when he went up the Amazon with some friends.

Jean found she could never be sure what kind of mood Peter would be in. Theirs was a strange relationship and one that, try as she might, she found difficult to accept. Indeed the only time she felt relaxed and happy was when he skilfully acted the part of a loving husband.

Meeting the mothers at school, delivering or fetching their children, helped Jean to make more friends. She was about the youngest wife and one of the few who had no children. Most of them had known Peter's sister and the children for several years and were sympathetic with Jean, recognising her problems, offering advice as to how to cope with them.

'It isn't easy with your own children,' Leila Tamson once said. 'It's a hundred times harder when they're not.'

The children, indeed, were a problem. Hugh, as Peter's mother had said, rarely spoke. He was polite and answered questions, but that was about all; he was obedient and went to bed when told it was time, but it worried Jean and she even talked to Peter about it. Peter had seemed annoyed.

'Leave the boy alone,' he said crossly. 'It's not easy for him to accept you in his mother's place.'

Jean felt hurt, but there was nothing she could say or do, for Peter was right in a way—yet shouldn't something to be done to help poor Hugh? she often wondered.

Nick was as spoilt as she had been warned. He even tried to bargain with her about going to bed, refusing to go unless he got a bar of chocolate. Peter overheard it one day and gave him a spanking—Nick went off howling loudly, but Jean noticed he stopped bargaining with her! Nick was always trying to stir up trouble, kicking Hugh suddenly, tugging at Vanessa's hair! Indeed the only time Hugh really spoke was when he lost his temper and shouted at his young brother.

Vanessa was a problem, too. Some days she would eat nothing, saying she was too fat already. Seeing she was about as thin as it was possible to be, that was nonsense. Peter frowned when Jean told him.

'She's only doing it to attract attention. Just let her starve. I bet she'll eat enough to make up for it tomorrow.'

As usual, Peter was right, but Jean still felt unhappy about it. When she reminded him of his promise of a little faraway room where the children could have the music as loud as they liked, Peter looked surprised.

'Sorry,' he said. 'I forgot about it. Tell Luke to get it made.'

Luke Whitwell, the farm manager, was amused at the request.

'I've no time for that kind of music myself,' he said. 'I don't blame Crosby for not wanting that noise in his house.'

'But young people do,' Jean told him.

The man smiled at her, his eyes amused. 'Don't tell me you do. Know something, Jean? I just can't believe you're twenty-two. You look younger than Vanessa.'

Jean had to laugh. 'I'm glad I'm not her age. It's a horrid age.'

'Were you like that?' he asked.

Luke Whitwell had become part of the family, frequently coming to eat with them, good at handling the children, baby-sitting when Peter took Jean out for the evening.

'I'm afraid so,' said Jean.

'Afraid of what?' Peter asked, surprising them both, for he had come into the room quietly.

'I was just saying that I'm afraid I was like Vanessa when I was her age,' Jean told him.

He looked at her thoughtfully, shrugged and turned away.

'Sometimes you still are,' he said, and left the room.

It was Luke who showed surprise, though Jean felt it.

'What was that about, Jean?' he asked.

She shrugged. 'I don't know. He's just in one of his moods.'

Luke stared at her. 'Most writers are temperamental.'

'He says he isn't a writer. He's a Professor of Economics—it's simply because he knows so much that he's been asked to write these books and now, quite suddenly, he's hating every moment of it,' Jean explained.

'Why did he take the job on, then?'

'I don't really know, but a . . .' She hesitated. It would be so easy to betray the truth— to tell Luke that the marriage was one of convenience only, that it had been arranged to keep the children out of his way. 'I think he was worried about the children. He felt they'd had enough shock losing both their parents and that it would be wrong to take them away from their home and send them to boarding school. The books meant he could come here to live for several years, and by then he . . . we'll be able to decide what's best for them.'

Luke nodded thoughtfully. 'Darned unselfish of you both. You happy here?'

'Oh yes!' Jean was startled at the question. 'I'm getting used to it and . . . well, it is a lovely place and . . well . . .' She hesitated again, afraid she might say too much and that the man sitting opposite her, his eyes narrowed thoughtfully as he stared, might learn too much about the strange relationship she had with Peter Crosby.

Under Luke's supervision a rondavel was built, far down in the garden. The planning was hilarious, for Luke insisted on the three children standing together and shouting at the top of their voices while Jean stood in Peter's study listening. Then she would go to the window and wave her hankie at them. Two waves meant she had heard them, three that she couldn't. It took quite a long time to make absolutely certain that not a single sound could reach Peter at his work.

To reach the rondavel they had to walk down the stone steps built into the mountainside. It was Jean's first trip and she could see the turgid slow-moving water of the river below. She felt a little shiver. Were there really crocodiles in it? she wondered. No one had mentioned them, but then it wasn't something you talked about unless some terrible accident happened. The children never went down to the river's edge. Bushes and trees crowded close to the water, luckily, leaving no temptation. The Tamsons had a swimming pool in their garden, so the children always went there if they wanted to swim.

The rondavel was quite big with a stable door and they soon furnished it from the farmhouse. Then they discovered something. Vanessa's record player was electric! Jean had to ask Peter if she could buy a record player run by battery. She went nervously, since he was not in a good mood. He had hardly spoken at lunch time, had frowned when Nick began to shout. Now as she went into his study, he looked up with a frown.

'What do you want?' His voice was almost aggressive.

'I'm sorry to worry you . . .' she began.

'Then why are you?'

She hesitated. 'I . . . the rondavel is ready, but . . . but we need a record player that's . . .'

'I know. Battery. Right?' he asked curtly. 'Okay, order one at Jundles. He'll get it up from Manzini.'

'You don't mind?' Jean was so surprised at his quick acceptance that she could hardly speak.

'Why should I?' he asked. 'I'm not quite an ogre.' He turned to the notes he was reading and she knew she was dismissed, but something held her back.

'Peter,' she said gently. Her cheeks went hot as she realised what she had said, for she never called him by his Christian name before except in public. 'Is something wrong?'

He looked up, scowling. 'Just about everything is wrong. These figures of Luke's . . . I just haven't time to check them.'

Again she hesitated. It was like balancing on the edge of a volcano, she thought. 'Could I . . . I mean, if I can do anything to help?'

She waited for his explosion, his contempt, his remark that she was too immature. Instead, he brushed his hand through his hair and looked at her.

'I haven't asked you as you seem pretty busy all day.'

'I could do it in the evenings when you're writing.'

He smiled, and Jean took a long breath. If only he would always smile, she thought. His whole stern face changed, the lines vanishing.

'Are you sure?'

'Quite sure. I'll be glad of something to do.' He stood up. 'That's fine.'

He collected a pile of papers, slid them into a long black book and passed them all to her. 'There's no hurry, you know, just that I want them out of the way.' He stared at her thoughtfully. 'Not that I'm suggesting Luke has made any mistakes. He's a good man. It's just I want to see what sort of an idiot my brother-in-law was. Some of their purchases were crazy, it seems to me. You said you liked Luke.'

'Yes . . . he's easy to get on with.'

Now Peter's eyes were amused. 'Easier than me?' he asked.

Jean hesitated and then nodded. 'Your mother warned me you'd be difficult,' she confessed.

He frowned. 'Am I?'

'You have moods.'

'You don't say?' Peter rubbed his hand through his hair again and sighed. 'I'm sorry, but this is one hell of a job. I wish I'd never taken it on. I just loathe this being pinned to a desk. My feet are itching to travel . . . I'm just not an office-sitting man. I was a fool to think it would work.' He sighed. 'Okay. Thanks,' he added, sorting out some papers.

This time Jean took the dismissal and went outside. On the *stoep*, she sat down, remembering what he had said. Wondering what he had meant—and how it might affect her.

'I wish I'd never taken it on,' he had said, meaning the writing job. 'My feet are itching to travel.' How long, then, could he stay in this out-of-the-world place, pinned, as he put it, to a desk? Yet was it a contract? Something he could not break? Then there was his last words:

'I was a fool to think it would work.'

What had he meant? What had he thought *would work*? Was he thinking of his writing—or was it of her?

Was she a failure? Were the children worrying him? Was that why he couldn't write? Was it because of her youth and lack of experience that she couldn't control the children and keep them out of his way?

Was that what he was regretting—his marriage of convenience to her? Was that the reason for his moods, his frustration? she asked herself. She closed her eyes quickly, determined not to let him see her in tears. Was it—could it be all *her* fault?

CHAPTER SIX

Two letters came for Jean the next day. One was from her mother and one addressed in Maggie's sprawling writing. Jean stood very still as she took them from the box at the post office, a small building tucked away between the two rival stores. The children were with her, for she had just picked them up at school after she had spent a morning in the garden of one of her new friends, drinking coffee and talking.

'Auntie Jean,' Nick shouted, 'I'm starving!'

'Coming!' she called, pushing the letters into her handbag and going out to the car.

The heat of the sunshine seemed to grow stronger every day—and as she drove along the road and then the track, she wondered how long it would be before the rainy season began. She rather dreaded that, though Peter had promised to help her and said there was always a tractor if she got stuck.

The night before, she had glanced through the notes, accounts and the black book Peter had given her. It certainly seemed as if Peter's brother-in-law had always been buying things, but then perhaps you had to on a farm? She had found a new interest in the farm itself which, up to now, she had ignored—at least as much as she could, for the noises of the tractors and the laughter and shouts of the farm workers made it pretty impossible. There were a few cows, so they never lacked milk, and hens which wandered around the flower garden but rarely laid eggs, judging from the number she had to buy, for the family all liked at least two eggs each for breakfast.

Vanessa was curled up on the car seat by Jean's side. 'Auntie Jean,' she said, and Jean immediately recognised the note in her voice. She wanted something! 'There's going to be a ball at the hotel quite soon and I want to go. All my friends are going, you see. It's sort of a family ball. Do you think Uncle Peter will create?'

Jean was busy avoiding hitting a small goat who had slithered down the side of the road, almost landing under the car wheels.

'I don't see why,' she said.

Vanessa smiled, 'Thanks!'

Several cows, eating grass on the verge, looked up as the car rounded a corner and deliberately and with an absurd look of insolence strolled across the road. Jean sighed, slowing up the car, waiting for a piccanin to come running to drive the cattle away.

'He hit me . . . he hit me!' screeched Nick from the back of the car.

Hugh didn't answer. She could imagine what he was doing, gazing blankly out of the car window at the cattle as if nothing stood in their way and nothing had happened.

If only, Jean thought wearily, if only she knew how to cope with the children, or were all children of this age like this? She tried to remember life at home . . . and that reminded her that there was a letter from her mother in her handbag. She shivered a little and then felt ashamed. Why was she always so afraid of her parents' reaction? She was six thousand miles away and . . .

It was not until after lunch that Jean had a chance to read the letters. Vanessa had been sent to her bedroom to do her homework—which meant Jean must go up every half hour and check that Vanessa *was* working and not reading one of the comics she liked. The two boys had gone out into the garden and, standing alone on the *stoep*, Jean opened her handbag, taking out the two letters.

She lay on the long canvas chair and looked at the letters. It was absurd, but she dreaded opening the one from her mother. They were, sure to be furious with her for marrying without telling them—and for not writing before. She knew now that if *she* was her mother, she would be very upset.

She opened Maggie's letter, knowing it was cowardly yet postponing what she would have to do eventually. Maggie's news was amazing.

She was going to be married!

'It's all your fault, Jeanie,' Maggie had written. 'You made me feel that, like you, I must break away from the boring life we led. The word Swaziland fascinated you— the name of a town, you must have read the book? *A Town Like Alice* has always intrigued me, and that's where we're going, Jock and I. In Australia, it will be such a different way of living, and Jock is sure we'll make a lot of money. Like you with Peter, I haven't known Jock long, yet there's something about him, something I can't pin down, but makes me feel I'd rather die than not go with him. We're funny creatures, aren't we? This love question is crazy—how can you know if you really love someone or not until you've been together for a long time? I hope things are going well with you and that your dream will come true. The wedding is next month. My family are horrified—they say we haven't known one another long enough!'

Maggie getting married and going to Australia! Jean found it hard to believe. Maggie had always said she wasn't going to marry until she was thirty, because marriage meant babies and nappies and doing things you don't like doing, and she wanted to enjoy herself.

'Help, help!' Nick's scream startled her. There was a reality about it, so she dropped her letters on the table and rushed outside.

She was beginning to recognise Nick's faked cries for help, but this was serious. Nick lay on the lawn, blood trickling down his cheeks, his eyes tightly closed as he screamed. Hugh stood by his side, his face still as a mask.

'What happened, Hugh?' Jean demanded.

'He tripped.'

Nick opened his eyes. 'He kicked me!' he shouted. Jean half smiled, looking at Hugh. 'I find that hard to believe. Did you, Hugh?'

Hugh turned to look at her. There was something pathetic about his expression. 'I didn't,' he muttered.

'I'm sure you didn't,' Jean said warmly, and was rewarded by another glance from Hugh. 'Look, Hugh, the first aid things are in the bathroom cupboard. Would you get them for me? I'll clean the cut . . .'

Nick was crying, but this time it was obvious that he was making a mountain out of a small mound. Maybe he had been frightened at the beginning, but as she bathed the wound, it turned out to be only a small cut. She bandaged it up, thinking that he might enjoy looking as if the wound was a big one, and then he went off, running outside.

As she went back to the *stoep*, she heard a door shut. She looked round. Could it be Peter's study door? she wondered. He must surely have heard the screams? Perhaps he had come out to investigate.

The letters were on the table as she had

102

left them—but had Maggie's been inside the envelope? Surely, Jean thought, in her hurry to go to find out what was wrong with Nick, she wouldn't have had time to put the letter in neatly? Could that mean that Peter . . .?

She sat down, re-reading the letter. Was there anything in it that could have told Peter the truth?

'Like you with Peter, I haven't known Jock long, yet there's something I can't pin down but makes me feel I'd rather die than not go with him . . .' Had Peter read that? Could he have thought that she had felt the same as Maggie? That there was something about Peter that made her willing to pay any price so long as she could stay with him? 'Oh no!' she thought. 'Peter wouldn't read it like that. The "Like you" could have to do with how long they had known one another . . .'

Feeling relieved, Jean opened her mother's letter. She was tense, prepared for angry reproachful words. But she got the reverse.

'We were delighted to hear that you had met the man of your dreams and married him. You were always the rebel in the family, Jean dear, surprising us, so we've got used to your sudden decisions. We're all delighted that you're so happy and the farm sounds beautiful. We're looking forward to seeing the snapshot of you all. What would you like for a wedding present, darling? Perhaps it would be wisest to send you a draft and then you could buy something you both want. Dad and I are talking of flying out to see you next year—that would be really nice. Love from us all. Celia is cross with you a little as she wanted to be your bridesmaid, but maybe she could be your first baby's godmother. She's crazy about children, as you know, and I'm only afraid she may marry some day simply to have babies. I'm sure that wasn't why *you* married your Peter. It was obvious in your letter that you adore him, practically every sentence you wrote was about Peter, as if he never left your thoughts. We're very pleased, darling, very pleased indeed.'

Well, I never did! Jean thought as she put down the letter. It was the surprise of her life. Her parents approved! Were pleased for her. Planned to come out to see them. Talked of her having a baby! If they knew the truth . . .

She folded the letter and put it back in its envelope, suddenly realising that had that been the letter she had first opened, it might have been the one on the table and Peter have read it. That was, of course, if Peter *had* read Maggie's letter. Somehow it didn't seem the kind of thing he would do.

But fancy her mother saying that the letter had shown them that their daughter loved this unknown man and was very happy. Was it so obvious? Jean wondered, suddenly afraid. Life would be unbearable if Peter knew the truth.

That evening Peter drove her down to the Club. He went off to his group of friends while she sat on a stool with hers. The chatter was loud, but it was all pleasant, because Peter would smile across the bar at her, or bring her a drink and ask if she was all right. She looked up at him and smiled, and when he smiled back, she could not believe that the expression in his eyes was faked. He couldn't dislike her and yet smile at her like that.

But driving back together in the car, her fantasy was destroyed.

'I hear Vanessa wants to go to the hotel ball,' he said curtly.

'She did mention it.' Jean was already sensing the change in him.

'She said that *you* said she could go,' Peter snapped.

'I didn't!' Jean sat up, twisting in the seat to look in his direction. 'I merely thought that if it was a family ball as she said it was, I didn't see why we couldn't all go.'

'You'd like to?'

Jean hesitated. She knew how he hated a whole evening away from the work he loathed but apparently must do. 'I thought if we could get a partner for Vanessa—Leila would know of someone—and went as a family, it might be rather fun.'

'Could be . . . Might even be an idea to make a party of it. I know several couples who might like to join us,' Peter said, surprising her. 'When is it?'

'I don't know. Do they dress up much here?

I mean, I haven't an evening dress, but I could make one—and one for Vanessa, too.'

'You can sew?' Peter sounded as if he didn't believe her.

'Of course I can. We had to buy our clothes out of our pocket money, so we made our own, it's much cheaper.'

'Is that so?' Peter's voice sounded as if he was amused. 'I wonder how Vanessa will react?'

'I wonder, too,' Jean confessed, frowning a little, as she thought ahead. Perhaps Vanessa would think a home-made evening dress was not "the thing"; perhaps the idea of being part of an adult party might also annoy her, for maybe she wanted to go with her own friends.

But Vanessa didn't take it that way. She just stared as if shocked by surprise as Peter said quietly at dinner that they were making a party of it and if she liked to join, she could.

'I can really go?' Vanessa's voice was full of surprise, followed by delight. 'How super-duper! Don't choose anyone young for me, Uncle Peter. I hate boys and much prefer men.'

'I see.' A smile he controlled made Peter's mouth tremble, Jean saw. 'There's the question of a dress. Jean is making herself one and said she'd make you one, too.'

'You would?' Vanessa's eyes seemed to widen. 'That would be smashing.'

'I thought tomorrow we'd ask at the Store if

they have patterns.'

'Oh, they do . . . and simply super material. A long dress, with sort of smocking . . . oh, Auntie Jean! Oh, that's terrific!'

Jean wasn't so sure next day as they went through the patterns available and tried not to listen to Nick's impatient shouts. They were in the one store that stayed open at all in the lunch hour, but it closed at half past one, so they hadn't much time. In the end, Jean had chosen a straight, sheath-like dress and some soft leaf-green silk. Vanessa couldn't make up her mind, so it was a last-minute decision of an Empire style dress with a high waistline, sleeveless and backless. The material was a mixture of green, yellow and pink, and held up against her the colour of the material certainly did something to the girl with her reddish hair and young face.

What with the accounts to go through, the book to check, Luke to talk to about the accounts, plus the dressmaking, the days flew by, so crowded with work were they. Vanessa was thrilled with her dress and kept trying it on, walking up and down in front of the mirror to make sure it was long enough.

At long last—according to Vanessa, it had seemed ages—the party met at the farmhouse, planning to drive down together. The partner for Vanessa looked as if his arm had been twisted by his aunt, his long hair curled on his pale pink shirt, his eyes bored, but Vanessa shone with excitement. Frank wasn't *old*, but he was at least seven years older than she was! Another couple drove up, came into the house and Peter introduced them.

'This is Louise Penton,' he began. 'Louise, this is Jean.'

Louise smiled, and Jean just stared, for never had she met anyone so beautiful, with long straight dark hair, slightly curled at the ends, her dark eyes warm with friendliness, her skin like a peach, her voice husky.

'Louise is staying with her uncle and aunt at Keppels farm. She's brilliant, been to an agricultural college, taught in schools, and has come to stay—we all hope for ever.' He smiled as he spoke.

Jean felt something cold go down her back. Peter was smiling at Louise as if she was something precious. How was it he knew her? Yet Jean had never met her?

'Don't, Peter!' Louise protested, laughing. 'You're always praising me, and I could get conceited.'

'Most unlikely,' he said with a smile.

Jean was hardly listening to him, for she was thinking of what Louise had said: 'You're always praising me.' Always? That meant they had met often? Why hadn't Peter talked about Louise? Why hadn't she met her? Jean was asking herself. Was this why he had said so angrily the other day that he had thought it would work but it hadn't? Was he regretting his marriage of convenience, wishing he had waited for someone like Louise, someone used to children, capable of running a farm alone, someone so attractive?

'What about me?' an amused deep voice asked.

Jean swung round. They were standing on the *stoep*, the moon high in the star-sparkling sky. A tall man stood waiting, a smile on his face. He had a pointed dark beard, sideboards and quite the friendliest voice Jean had ever heard. He held out his hand.

'Maybe I'd better introduce myself. I'm David Fox. Glad to meet you, Jean,' he said with a smile.

As she felt his hand close round hers, some of Jean's dismay vanished. Maybe she was imagining it all, she thought.

'Let's get going,' said Peter 'You can take my wife, David, and the rest can come with me.'

'Suits me,' David said with a laugh. 'Come on, Jean. We've a lot to talk about.'

'We have?' She hesitated, but he had taken hold of her hand, and as Peter had said she was to go with this stranger, it might be wiser to do so. It was obvious that Peter wanted to be with Louise. Very obvious indeed, Jean thought miserably.

'Yes,' David was saying gaily. 'I come from the Isle of Man, too,' he began, but his words slowly died away, for he could see that she was not listening.

*   *   *

The hotel was bright with colour, with huge vases of beautiful flowers, even the trees that shielded the terrace from the sun during the days were now decorated with coloured lights.

It was a pleasant evening in some ways, Jean thought as she danced in David's arms. Peter was acting as the perfect husband, making sure she was happy, and then vanishing, to be seen a little later dancing with Louise! The floor was crowded. It was a real 'family' ball with fathers dancing with the daughters of their friends and middle-aged women looking breathless but thrilled as they were whirled around by their friends' sons. Vanessa seemed to be having a good time, although her partner, Frank, was seldom with her, but Vanessa was obviously enjoying her chance to dance with 'older men'.

After a while, David suggested they had a drink outside, as it would be cooler. Jean agreed. But it wasn't much cooler. It was a perfect African night with warm air, a gentle breeze causing the leaves of the trees to rustle, the dark sky with the very bright stars shining and the full moon reflecting in the dam below.

'It's beautiful,' she said as they sat down at one of the tables and a waiter in his white suit and little red fez brought them drinks.

'You like it here?' David asked casually.

'Very much . . .' she began, and paused. 'Sometimes,' she added.

'The children must be rather a handful.'

She laughed. 'They are, sometimes. Also Peter thinks I'm soft with them and I think he's harsh.'

'I think most parents are like that.' David looked thoughtful. 'It can't be an easy relationship, particularly when the children are not your own. You'll probably find it easier when the children are.'

Jean was glad it was not light where they sat, for she felt her cheeks beginning to burn. Were they all watching her, waiting for the first sign that she was pregnant? If they only knew the truth—that there was no danger of that! That was the worst of a small community—you were watched all the time and discussed and gossiped about. The longer she was there the more she understood why Peter had suggested the marriage, for she could imagine the acid discussions there would have been about Peter Crosby and his 'governess'.

The music drifted out through the open doors, voices came, laughter, but few couples had sought the beauty of the evening outside.

'Have you been here long?' she asked.

'Long enough to have fallen in love with the country and its people,' he said with a laugh. 'It's something you either love or hate. Unfortunately Peter's sister hated it—but then she wasn't like you.'

'Like me?'

David nodded, 'You're happily married—that's obvious from the way Crosby behaves. I'm afraid poor Dorothy wasn't.'

'What do you do?' Jean asked. She was right, then, she thought, and Peter was one of the best actors! Happily married! She wasn't sure if she wanted to laugh or to cry.

'I'm at the Research Station. Interesting work . . .' David began.

'Oh, there you are, Jean.' Peter's voice interrupted. He sounded annoyed. 'I've been looking for you.'

'Hi,' David said with a grin. 'Sorry about that. We thought it might be cooler outside.'

'And is it? Peter sat down opposite them, easing his collar. He stretched his legs. 'Never danced so much in all my life. That girl never seems to get tired.'

'What girl?' David asked.

'Louise, of course. Unusual to find a beautiful girl with brains.'

'And a hard worker, too. She's not sure how long she'll stay.'

'She's going to help us. I know nothing about farming, so she's going to discuss it with Luke.' Peter turned and smiled at Jean. 'Good of her, isn't it.'

'Very good,' Jean managed to say, but she found herself battling with the desire to say 'Charming' as Maggie would have done in a sarcastic voice. So Louise was going to take over the farm, as well as Peter and Luke!

She stood up and murmured something, hurrying into the hotel to the powder room. There was no doubt—no doubt at all in her mind but that Peter fancied this Louise. How he must be wishing he'd not plunged into this marriage of convenience, for Louise would have made the perfect foster-mother for the children, manager of the farm and Peter's wife! How mad Peter must feel, how angry with himself.

Vanessa came in. 'Isn't it super?' she asked, going to the mirror to add shadow to her eyes and powder to her nose. 'It really is great, isn't it?'

'Yes—it is great,' Jean agreed, trying to sound sincere.

Driving home much later, Peter was silent. It was Vanessa who chatted away, talking of the different men she had danced with.

'And they all think I'm eighteen or nineteen,' she said proudly. 'So I let them!' she laughed.

Peter vanished as soon as they reached home, going into his study. Even at that hour, Jean thought.

'You did enjoy it, Aunt Jean?' Vanessa asked, a little note of anxiety in her voice.

Jean forced a smile. 'Of course. It's just I'm a bit tired now.'

'See you in the morning.' Vanessa almost

danced down the corridor to her bedroom, looking happier than Jean had ever seen her.

Alone in her room Jean gazed in the mirror. She did look miserable, she thought. Somehow she must find a way of accepting what lay ahead for whatever happened, Peter mustn't ever know how much she loved him.

*   *   *

The next day she awoke to weather that matched her mood. The usually cloudless sky was grey and thick with low clouds, the rain pouring down—not the fine rain she was used to but heavy rain. Peter vanished as usual and the children squabbled and Vanessa spent most of the time on the phone, telling her friends about the wonderful time she had had.

Jean rang Luke and asked him up and discussed the accounts with him and tried to learn more about the farm. Apparently it had never been a success. Dorothy's husband had been keen on trying new ideas and spending money he could ill afford.

'When I took over after the accident, it was quite a nightmare,' Luke said slowly. 'I wondered how I'd ever make order out of the chaos. He didn't keep proper accounts or anything. However, things began to improve and now that Peter has backed us up financially, I think we should do quite well.'

Luke told her about the cotton harvest, the

last-minute fears of hail coming, the many hazards.

'Actually when you look at it sanely, you wonder why anyone is a farmer. No matter how hard you work, how careful you are, you're at the mercy of the elements. A sudden storm—or a season with little rain . . . there are so many things that you're fighting. Yet,' he sighed, twirling his cigarette in his hand, looking down at it with a frown, 'yet I wouldn't want any other job.'

They were sitting on the *stoep*, watching the way the distant mountains were vanishing in the heavy rain and looking at the long twisting small streams that were destroying the flower beds as the water ran through the garden.

'I suppose it's something like living here, you either love or hate it,' Jean said slowly.

Luke chuckled. 'I hear you've been talking to David? He's back from his holiday, is he?'

'Yes, he came to the ball last night with us.'

'And Louise?' Luke's voice changed 'She's quite a dish, isn't she?' There was a wistful note in his voice that made Jean look at him.

'You've met her?' she asked.

'She was here six months ago and went away. I didn't know she was back,' he said almost curtly as if he didn't want to discuss it.

Jean was puzzled, for Louise had said 'You're always praising me' to Peter, so when had he seen her? Or had he driven into town when the children were at school and Jean drinking endless cups of coffee in the gardens of her various friends—and had he met Louise there?

'Peter said she was going to ask you about the farm,' Jean began.

'That's not what I said,' Peter told her, suddenly appearing at one of the open windows that led to the rooms within the house. 'I said she was going to discuss it with Luke. Why do you always twist my words, Jean?' he asked.

'I didn't mean to.'

'I'm aware of that,' he said coldly. 'Maybe one day you'll grow up.' He closed the window.

There was a stillness between Jean and Luke that could almost be heard. Then Luke spoke. 'What's the matter with him these days? He's always having moods.'

'I know.' Jean hesitated, but went on. 'I think he's wishing he hadn't accepted the commission of writing those books. He never says why . . . I mean why he hates writing them now or . . . or . . . anything.' She was horrified to hear her voice trembling and stood up. 'I'll tell Violet to make us some coffee,' she said, and hurried inside.

She had thought it was the writing of the books that Peter was hating, as it was not his usual work, but now she knew what was really troubling him. It was so plain: since he had met Louise he had realised what a terrible mistake he had made in marrying a young—to him—English girl who was useless in her job, because she found it impossible to keep the children out of his way and knew nothing about farming. If only she *did* know . . . perhaps the library would have some books, but then with Louise about . . . The children, too . . .

After speaking to Violet in the kitchen, Jean heard Nick screaming and hurried to their playroom. Nick was on his back, kicking his legs in the air, while Hugh was curled up on the window-seat, reading a book.

'What's wrong?' she asked.

Nick sat up. 'He hates me . . . he said so!' Nick pointed a finger at Hugh, who was taking no notice at all. 'He won't play with me!'

'Now what's going on?' Peter asked, coming up behind Jean.

Nick's eyes widened. 'Nuffin.'

'But something must be wrong to make you scream like that,' Peter told him.

Nick looked frightened, gazing round the room like a captured wild animal. 'Hugh won't play with me.'

'He was playing earlier this morning, wasn't he? You can't expect him to play all the time,' said Peter, sounding annoyed. 'What did you want to play?'

'Table tennis. I wanta play . .' Nick began to wail again, but seeing Peter's quick frown stopped.

Jean stifled a sigh. How did you deal with

such a child? Nick had been spoilt all his life, now no one was spoiling him. Was it good for him to have to face up to the truth—that he was no longer a spoilt baby? Peter was frightening him.

'I wouldn't mind a game,' Peter said surprisingly. 'Come on, Nick.'

Nick's startled face relaxed into a smile. 'I'm coming,' he said, and scrambled to his feet and led the way to the other end of the room where there was a small table with a net over it.

Hugh was still reading, but Jean had noticed he hadn't turned over a single page since she had come into the room. That was how he retreated. Poor Hugh, she thought, if only she could find a way to get through to him.

She left the room where Nick's shouts of delight filled the air and went back to the *stoep*. Luke had gone—not far, though, for with his mackintosh over his head he stood in the rain as he spoke to the girl in the small red car, who was laughing. She looked over his shoulder and saw Jean standing on the *stoep* and waved to her.

'Hi!' Louise shouted. 'I thought this was a good chance to see Luke. We're going to his office.'

Luke turned and waved goodbye, then got into the car which Louise drove down the slope towards Luke's small house. Jean stood alone, suddenly afraid she had lost Luke's friendship as well as Peter's. Louise was

118

beautiful, brilliant and clever. She knew how to catch a man.

CHAPTER SEVEN

The next two weeks were like a nightmare. It rained as Jean had never seen it rain before—more like cloudbursts, she thought one day as she drove the children to school. It was hard to see through the windscreen even though the wipers were working like mad.

Would she ever forget that first day? she wondered. Peter had driven them to school, and on the way home Jean had been given the wheel. It was an entirely new way of driving, thick mud she must avoid and sudden skids when the car moved sideways. He kept telling her what to do, but somehow she never seemed to do it right, and frequently he had to grab the wheel and help her out of the mess she was in. He had been very patient with her, but with the controlled exasperated voice of a schoolteacher.

'I'm sorry I'm so slow at it,' she apologised as they reached the farm.

He had given an odd smile. 'You'll grow used to it.'

But driving back to the school alone to fetch the children had been a real nightmare as she tried in vain to remember what he had taught her. Fortunately the track was wide, so there was no question of the car sliding over the edge of a mountain to fall thousands of feet, but all the same, she didn't want to get stuck and have to be rescued.

The second day had been slightly better, as the rain was not so heavy, though the ruts were soft with thick mud. Most of the mothers let the children race across the yard to the school and had driven away, though one or two waved invitingly to Jean, but she put her hand to her head and they nodded, guessing she meant she had a headache—which was untrue, but she had a strong desire to get back to the farm, even though it meant two journeys instead of one.

Later she saw that her intuition had been right, for as soon as she returned there was Louise's little red car, parked by the house. Jean had hesitated, wondering if it would be wiser to turn back and drive to Manbina, for she didn't want to be in the way—but after all, if Peter wanted to be with Louise, he had a perfect right to be with her and he would certainly not allow Jean's presence to interfere. So why worry? she asked herself.

She went to her room, but the bed was not made yet nor the room cleaned, so back she went to the *stoep* again, reading a book yet not seeing a single word . . . Where was Louise? she asked herself. Was she with Luke? If so, wouldn't her car have been parked down at

Luke's house? Surely as the car was here, so was Louise?

Violet brought out tea and a few moments later Jean heard Louise's voice in the corridor in the house. Jean didn't move, but she heard the study door open and then laughter. Had Violet told them that Jean was sitting outside alone on the *stoep*? If they had, it made no difference, for no one appeared. Jean felt terrible, which was, she knew, absurd. This was a marriage of convenience, she told herself again and again. Peter was not to be blamed at all. He had never pretended it was more than a marriage in name only, so there was no reason why he couldn't have a girl-friend. Had he told Louise? she wondered. The thought made her feel uncomfortable—she could imagine Louise's laughter and probably her question as to what kind of girl would take such a job! It had been an unhappy twenty minutes before Jean had driven back to the school. If she was too early, she would wander round the stores, for they often had some delightfully colourful squares of material which would make gorgeous long evening dresses.

Now as she thought back remembering how Louise often stayed to lunch with them, joking with the children yet somehow handling them with a skill Jean envied. The first lunch was merely a start, for Louise began to turn up at odd hours, apologising but saying her uncle was not feeling well and she felt in the way there and she hoped they didn't mind. Always Peter laughed and said of course they didn't—indeed, it was a blessing, as it helped Jean, who hadn't Louise's knack with the youngsters.

'I'm right, aren't I, Jean?' he had asked once.

Jean wanted to howl, though it was the truth. 'Quite right,' she said quietly. 'I wish I had.'

Louise smiled, a friendly smile. 'It takes time, Jean. Don't forget I've taught children, so I'm used to them. In any case, it's easier for me, an outsider, to handle them than their aunt. You know how kids are—always against what is called Establishment, which simply means anyone with authority. I guess we all go through that stage when we're young.'

How Peter had laughed, Jean was thinking as she rounded a sharp corner, and the car went deep into mud. Yes, he *had* laughed and laughed, and then he had said: 'Jean knows all about that, because she's only just getting over it as she grows up. Am I right, Jean?'

Jean's cheeks had burned, but she managed a laugh.

'Right as usual, Peter,' she said gaily, made an excuse and left the room, to stand in her bedroom, hands pressed against her face. Why must he say things like that in front of Louise? How old was Louise anyhow? She couldn't be more than twenty-six or seven. That wasn't so very much older than twenty-two—so why did

Peter keep harping about her age? Jean asked herself miserably.

'We've stuck!' Vanessa shouted.

'What?' With a jerk Jean left her memories of the past and returned to the present as she pressed the accelerator and the wheels turned but the car didn't move. She tried to reverse. It was hopeless.

'I'm hungry!' Nick began to wail.

'Why did you drive into the mud?' Vanessa asked angrily as if Jean had done it on purpose.

'I'm not used to driving on this kind of road,' Jean began.

'It happens to everyone,' Hugh said quietly. 'I've known it happen to Dad many times.'

Jean turned to him gratefully, amazed and pleased with the knowledge that he had defended her, mentioned his dead father, and had broken his long silence. This was the first time he had spoken like that; before he had merely answered questions.

'What do we do, then?' she asked.

Hugh opened his satchel and took out a book. 'Uncle Peter will guess why we're late and send out a tractor. That's what always happens,' he said.

'Good. I'm glad I'm not alone, Hugh. It's better to be with someone who knows what to do,' she said. Inside her, she was bubbling with joy. Hugh was talking! Something she had worried about all the time. Was this the secret,

123

perhaps? To ask his advice, to turn to him for help, to make him feel responsible and strong? Was that the way to help him?

'I'm hungry!' Nick wailed.

'Haven't you got a comic?' Hugh asked. 'Here's one.' He burrowed in his satchel and took one out and gave it to Nick. 'Read that and you'll forget you're hungry.'

Jean found it hard to believe, for Hugh was talking like any normal person. Vanessa was looking cross as she stared out of the car window at the grey rain pounding down on the huge stones and the thick mud.

At long last the tractor arrived, and towed them out of the mud. It was a slow business, but the two Swazis finally made it.

'We drive ahead of them and they follow,' Hugh directed. 'Then they pull us out again if we get stuck.'

'Thanks,' Jean said, and began to drive carefully along the wide track. Her joy at Hugh's change made her fear vanish and she wanted to sing.

'Can you drive, Hugh?' she asked.

'Dad taught me. I used to drive round the farm.'

'Then why not now?' Jean asked. 'Next weekend take me for a drive round the farm.'

'Could I?' he asked eagerly.

'He's not old enough,' said Vanessa.

'Not where there's traffic,' Jean agreed. 'But round the farm, he could.'

It was a slow difficult journey with the tractor making its way noisily behind her, but at last they reached the house, and raced through the rain to the shelter of the *stoep*. Peter came to meet them.

'Get stuck?' he asked.

'She went straight into the mud,' Vanessa said.

'That's a bad corner,' said Hugh. 'Dad often got stuck there.'

Jean saw the surprise in Peter's eyes as Hugh spoke, and later that day, when she was alone with Peter, she seized her chance.

'I was amazed. Hugh defended me in the car when Vanessa accused me of bad driving. I think we should make him feel . . . well, helpful.' She told Peter about Hugh's ability to drive. 'Could I let him drive me? I think it would help him so much.'

Peter smiled. 'Only on the farm? Right. I think it's a good idea. We might even teach him to drive a tractor.'

'That would really thrill him,' Jean said warmly.

'Oh, I think we may be able to help him after all.'

'It's young Nick that's the real problem. I think he needs a good spanking, but Louise doesn't agree.' Louise, as usual, Jean thought miserably. She seemed to dominate their lives.

'What does she think we ought to do?' she asked. Peter shrugged. 'She says Nick should be cuddled a lot, should feel we love him and . . .'

'But we have tried to, Peter. It's just that he wants his own way all the time. I don't see how we can give him that.'

'For once,' Peter said dryly, 'we agree.'

Jean turned away quickly, hoping he hadn't seen the hurt look on her face.

'One thing,' Peter went on, 'I've discovered that my brother-in-law was teaching both the boys to play chess. Can you play?'

'Goodness, no!' Jean was startled. She moved to straighten a crooked picture on the wall. 'Why?'

'Well, the boys are going to teach me. Luckily Louise can play, so I can always ask her advice . . .'

Is there anything Louise can't do? Jean wanted to shout at him. She was sick and tired of that name—Louise this, Louise that . . . She found herself trembling and clung to the back of a chair.

Peter had turned away and was looking out of the window at some cattle being driven along. 'Louise seems to think I'm making a mistake by keeping myself what she calls aloof. She says I must take over the part of a father.'

Jean stared at him. 'But . . .' she began.

'I know. I'm not their father, but she says I should show more interest in them, share their problems.'

'But your books? I mean, that's what you

wanted, to have someone to keep the children out of your way,' Jean protested.

Was Louise blaming *her*, she wondered, for keeping the children away from their uncle?

'Louise says the children are more important than my books,' Peter said slowly. 'She may be right.' He looked round suddenly. 'Do you think I seem an ogre to them?'

'Nick . . . Nick is, a bit scared of you, but . . .'

'You think it a good thing?' Peter, asked. When she nodded, he gave a wry smile. 'Louise doesn't agree. I must win Nick's trust, she said. Explain to him why he may do certain things and why he may not do others.'

'Well, I do that,' Jean said quickly, 'but it doesn't get me anywhere. Nick just doesn't want to listen, he wants to be a baby, his mother's darling . . .'

She wished she hadn't said that, for she saw the pain on Peter's face and knew how he hated hearing his sister criticised.

'Louise says that it's quite normal to spoil the youngest and that the middle child has the hardest time. That's why Hugh has been so difficult. Still, I think things will be better now we have Louise to advise us. I mean, that was pretty wonderful the way Hugh defended you and mentioned his father, too.'

'Yes,' Jean murmured, longing to shout at him: 'I suppose that was due to Louise, too. Everything is due to Louise, I'm just a nobody, a nuisance . . .' She found she was trembling with anger and the desire to say she was sick to death of the word *Louise*—but what good would it do her? It might even antagonise Peter still more, for he obviously thought Louise was wonderful.

'Is something wrong, Jean?' Peter asked. 'You're very quiet and you look pale.'

'Do I?' She was startled; if there was anything wrong, it was the angry resentment that filled her.

'Maybe it's this rain and the ordeal it obviously is for you to drive in this weather. Don't worry. I can do it, or if I'm busy, I know Louise would always drive in to fetch them. If you're feeling off colour, for goodness' sake say so, Jean. Now we've got Louise, she can take over the kids to give you a rest.'

'She has her own work,' Jean said.

Peter chuckled. 'That was just a cover-up. She left here six months ago in a flaming temper over something or somebody, then wanted to come back, but, so as not to lose face, she said her uncle needed her. It's the last thing he wants, because they argue all the time—that's why she escapes to us.'

Jean's eyes were narrowed. 'Louise had a big quarrel? But she's so . . .'

'Exactly. You wouldn't think it to see or listen to her.' He chuckled. 'She's a girl of many moods. She'll stand no nonsense, she'll speak her mind—a girl with a personality all her own,' he finished, his voice almost proud, Jean thought. 'I think we're lucky to have met her. Don't you?'

He was staring at her, Jean saw, his eyes puzzled as if her behaviour amazed him. Somehow she forced down the truth she wanted to say; somehow, too, she forced a smile on her face.

'Yes, we are lucky,' she agreed, and let herself yawn. 'I think I'll go to bed early. Good-night,' she said quickly, and hurried away.

*　　*　　*

Jean opened her eyes in the morning and saw the amazing miracle that so often happens in Africa, for one day the sky is grey with clouds that seem to threaten the ground below, while rain gushes down from the sky relentlessly, and then, a few hours later, the sky is cloudless and blue, the sun beams down and the rain has gone. She couldn't believe it at first and jumped out of bed, went to the window and drew back the curtains.

It was true! The sun was shining! And already the thick mud outside was drying. The dogs were racing round as if enjoying the sudden warmth and a tall Swazi, powerfully built and wearing a skin skirt, was beginning to work in the garden where so many plants had hung their heads under the weight of the rain.

Suddenly she wanted to laugh, to sing, to dance. One of her problems had been solved. Now there would be no reason for Peter or Louise to drive the children to and from school . . . now it would still be her job, Jean thought happily, for she had dreaded the humiliation of having to admit that she couldn't cope with the rain and the mud.

It was as if the sunshine was a symbol in her life, for suddenly everything seemed to change. As she drove the children to school, delighting in the warmth of the sunshine, for once they didn't fight or argue. Vanessa chatted away about a wonderful idea one of her friends had had.

'We plan to go camping. Near the Mantenga Falls, I think it is. Anyhow, there'd be about ten of us and it would be good fun,' Vanessa said happily, and then looked quickly at Jean. 'Will Uncle Peter let me go, do you think? Can you talk him into it? Like you did with the ball.'

'I didn't.' Jean was thinking how lovely it was to drive with no mud to send her skidding sideways, even though the deep ruts were something of a trial, too, it was nothing like as bad as it had been before.

'Oh yes, you did,' Vanessa beamed. 'You're on my side,' she added happily.

Jean hesitated. There should be no sides really. 'I just said I thought it would be fun if we all went.'

Vanessa laughed. 'Very clever of you, Aunt Jean. Try to think up a good reason why I should go camping!'

They had to slow up at a crossing and Nick began complaining that he was hungry. 'You've just had breakfast, Nick,' Jean reminded him.

'I'm starving,' he said mournfully. 'I'd like some chocolate.'

Jean hesitated again Should she buy him chocolate whenever he wanted it? Yet Louise had said he must be fussed over and loved.

'All right,' she said. 'We'll stop on the way.'

Of course the stores weren't open, as it wasn't even eight o'clock, so Nick was even more hungry, according to what he said. As they reached the school, the tall man with a dark beard and a friendly smile came to meet them. It was David Fox.

'Hi, Jean,' he greeted her. 'I hoped to meet you here.' He smiled at Vanessa. 'How you doing? You enjoyed that ball? It was fun, wasn't it?'

Vanessa beamed. 'It was smashing, Uncle David. When are we going to have another?'

'I'm hungry,' Nick said wistfully.

'The stores aren't open yet,' Jean began,but David spoke as well.

'Hungry? What about some chocolate?' He put his hand in his pocket and pulled out a packet, solemnly bent it into three and handed one part to each of the children.

Nick's face shone. 'Thanks!' He grabbed his and raced indoors. The other two thanked him more politely and then hurried to join their friends.

'Somewhat of a problem?' David asked. 'Young Nick, I mean.'

'He is. The latest is that we're not giving him enough love and that Peter is acting like an ogre.'

David smiled. 'And is he?'

'He's quite strict at times, but then ...'

David glanced at his watch and then up at the sky.

'What a lovely day! It seems a crime to have to be indoors. Look, Jean, I was hoping to see you and wondered if you'd come up to the hotel and have coffee with me? I've got a phone call to England booked—it's personal, so I didn't want to take it at the office, but I ought to start moving. How about it?'

'I'd love to,' Jean said, and meant it. As she got into the car and followed David's along the winding road, then to the plateau that was perched on the side of the mountain and above the new dam, she was thinking what an easy person he was to talk to. Somehow she always felt relaxed with him, at ease, not watching everything she had to say.

It was indeed pleasant to sit at a table on the terrace, while the waiter came with a smile and took the order. Suddenly the cicadas began their shrill song, a song that in time could grow

132

monotonous and annoying—then just as if someone had switched off, they were quiet, the stillness suddenly strong, and the birds began to sing as if it was their turn to have the stage.

'Well?' David asked with a smile. 'How are things doing?'

'I'm glad the rain's over.'

'It's not over, I'm afraid, but it may be some time before it returns. Your road must have been pretty bad.'

'I was terrified,' Jean admitted, and laughed. 'Honestly, I've never known anything like it. Yesterday I got stuck and felt so ashamed.'

'But that's absurd. Anyone can get stuck. Even Peter Crosby,' he added, his voice changing slightly.

Jean was puzzled. Didn't he like Peter? she wondered.

'I'm glad the sun is out,' she went on, really to change the subject.

'By the way,' David's voice was casual, 'seen Louise lately?'

'Oh yes,' Jean said quickly—too quickly, perhaps. 'She's up at our place a lot.'

'She is?' David sounded surprised. 'I thought that was . . .' The coffee arrived at that moment, so he didn't finish his sentence. Jean poured it out carefully, forgetting David's question for a moment, but he continued, 'What's she doing up there?'

'Helping us,' said Jean, trying to keep her voice natural when really she wanted to be sarcastic and catty. 'Advising Luke about the farm and . . .'

'Advising Luke? Why, that's crazy! He's one of the best farmers in the district,' said David. He was watching Jean's face. 'She's up there a lot, is she? Louise, I mean.'

'It seems she's not very happy with her uncle and . . . and so she comes to us.'

'How delightful for you all,' David drawled, and this time his sarcasm was clear. 'How do you feel about it?'

'How do I feel?' Jean began, and paused, suddenly remembering that she was supposed to be the loving wife of a perfect husband. 'Actually she is a help, David, because she's very good with the children. Much better than I am. Sometimes I seem to be getting nowhere, but a wonderful thing happened yesterday . . .' She leaned forward, resting her chin on her hands, her dark hair swinging forward, her face happy as she told him how Hugh had defended her when Vanessa accused her of careless driving. 'Honestly, we just couldn't make him talk. He would answer questions politely but never say a word. We were really thrilled.'

'I can imagine,' David smiled. 'Kids are problems, aren't they?'

'Well, ours are,' she admitted.

'It'll be different when they're your own,' David told her. 'What sort of family do you plan?'

Far a moment Jean just gazed at him silently. What sort of a family? She wanted to laugh and to cry at the same time, because there was nothing she would like more than to have Peter's child. 'We haven't really discussed it,' she said a little stiffly.

David gave her an odd look, then stood up. 'I think that must be my call. I won't be long,' he said.

Jean nodded. She was the only one on the terrace with the expanse of well-cared-for grass ahead of her, slanting slightly as the grass went down towards the dam. She was fascinated by one of the trees. It was a strange shape, something like a fir tree yet entirely different.

'Hullo, what are you doing here?' a voice asked.

Startled, Jean looked round. It was Amelia Franks, one of her friends and one of the youngest wives and mothers in the district.

'Just having coffee. Join us?'

Amelia, small, slim and full of energy in her white trouser suit, chuckled. 'I shan't be in the way?' She laughed. 'I mean, I hate playing gooseberry.'

'Gooseberry?' Jean asked, puzzled.

'Yah . . . didn't I see David just now?'

'Yes, I'm having coffee with him. He's waiting for a phone call to England.'

'Is he now?' Amelia smiled and sat down. 'I bet you're glad to see the sun.'

'I most certainly am,' Jean agreed.

'By the way. I keep meaning to ask you out to my house,' Amelia went on. 'How about coming now, or will David be mad?'

'Mad? Oh, mad! Of course not. I expect he's got to go back to the Research Station. He's only taking his call here because it's a personal one.'

'I wonder who it's to,' Amelia began.

'My mother,' David said, his voice crisp with annoyance. 'She's ill in hospital and I can't speak to her, but I talked to her doctor.'

Amelia looked startled. 'I'm sorry. Is it serious?'

'As serious as it can be,' he said grimly. 'Satisfied for the grapevine?' He turned to Jean. 'Mind if I rush off, Jean? I want to get back to the Station to see someone. Nice meeting you. Tell Peter there's something I want to ask him.'

'Come to dinner tonight?' Jean asked, hastily thinking of what lay in the deep-freeze and what they could eat.

He nodded. 'Thanks. Be seeing you, then. 'Bye.' He went off, waving his hand, and there was a little silence at the table.

'What's that funny-looking tree called?' Jean asked.

'Which? Oh, that one.' Amelia nodded. 'Monkey puzzle. Coming along with me now he's gone?'

'I'd love to. I'm not going home this

morning, but I'll just wait for the children to come out of school.'

'Good—then we can have a real natter. I'll drive ahead, or do you want to do some shopping first?'

'I'll do it on the way back,' said Jean.

She drove down the road behind Amelia's car. It was quite a way, through masses of trees, but finally they came out in the open and there ahead was the house—a beautiful one, Jean thought, mentally comparing it with her temporary home. Typical of the country, with the *stoep* running right round the building and the thatched roof.

Soon they were sitting on the *stoep* drinking coffee and chatting. Amelia seemed interested, asking many questions. How had Jean met Peter—was she an intellectual, too—did she mind being guardian of another woman's children, difficult children too, so it was said. Was she happy here—wasn't she bored after living in London—how long were they to stay? The questions seemed endless, but Jean answered them, a little wary in case she might say the wrong thing and let Amelia know the truth about the marriage of convenience. When Jean was tired of the questions, she looked at the beautiful garden with its blaze of scarlet and yellow flowers, bushes covered with purple or blue flowers—some she recognised, such as clematis and honeysuckle, but a lot were unknown to her.

'Does the river go through your garden?' she asked. 'It goes through ours at the bottom, but I haven't been down to see it.'

'You haven't?' Amelia asked, pouring out some fresh coffee.

Jean laughed, glad she had changed the conversation.

'Well, Peter told me there'd be crocodiles at the bottom of the garden and I didn't like the idea. They have such a horrible menacing sort of look.'

It was Amelia who laughed this time. 'You're scared of them? Are you scared of much here?'

'I don't like the mosquitoes or the heavy rain—and it was really quite cold when we first came out. I had an idea that it was never cold in Africa.'

'We have frost here, at least we do on the mountains. Black frost, sometimes, also hail that destroys the harvest at the last moment. Weather is our greatest enemy, because we can't control it.'

'That's what Luke says.'

'Luke Whitwell? He's quite a fellow. How do you get on with him, and how does Peter?'

'Very well indeed. He's a hard worker.'

'He's had to be. A real mess it was before he took over. You knew Peter's sister?'

'No.'

'A strange person—the kind who would be unhappy anywhere, but I must say she had a terrible husband. He was handsome, right, but where money was concerned he was crazy. David, he's another womaniser, so watch out, Jean.'

'David?' Jean was startled. 'I thought what a nice easy-going man he is.'

'Easy-going is the right word. You know, they say . . .' Amelia began, but Jean was suddenly tired of the gossip Amelia obviously wanted to tell her, so she looked at her watch.

'I really must go. I've a lot of shopping to do. Thanks for the coffee . . .'

'You must come again,' Amelia smiled.

Jean drove away, rather faster than usual. She had the oddest kind of feeling—that she shouldn't have talked so much to Amelia. Was that why David had snapped and said 'Satisfied?' and then mentioned the grapevine? She tried to remember all they had discussed and talked about, wondering if she could have betrayed the truth: the kind of marriage it was and the real love she felt for Peter. That would be the final humiliation if everyone was to learn that.

Louise also accepted the invitation to dinner that evening which Peter immediately suggested when Jean told him she had asked David. They had the usual prawn cocktails, then roast chicken with various vegetables, followed by fruit and cream.

'Very nice, Jean,' David said afterwards.

'We've a good cook called Dorcas,' Peter

explained. 'We're lucky that way.'

Jean glanced at him quickly and then away. Why had he to say nasty little things like that? she wondered. Suggesting, wasn't he, that it was a good thing they had a cook or they would all have starved.

Sitting outside in the warm night, they all talked, mostly about their work. Everyone was interested if Peter could be persuaded to tell them of some of his adventures in South America.

Jean was startled when suddenly Louise turned to her.

'So you haven't seen a crocodile yet?'

'No. Why?'

Louise, looking even more beautiful than ever, shrugged.

'No reason, I just wondered why. Seems you're scared of them?'

'How can she be scared of something she's never seen?' David asked.

Peter was laughing. 'She certainly is. I remember right at the beginning, when I told her there were crocodiles at the bottom of the garden, that she was quite upset. Weren't you, Jean?' he asked.

Watch out, Peter, she was thinking worriedly. Watch out or you'll be telling them how you spoke on the television, how you interviewed me, how I said I was afraid I would turn and run away . . . watch out.

'Weren't you, Jean?' Peter persisted.

Her face felt stiff as she managed to smile. 'Yes, I was. I think they give me the creeps, sliding along so slowly.'

'Know what they do when they catch someone?' Peter asked. 'They have a sort of shelf under water, put the body there and don't eat it until it's bad.'

'Peter, please! It makes me feel sick,' Jean protested, suddenly angry. Why must he always make her look a fool? 'Everyone has something they're scared of. I bet even you.'

'Touché.' David joined in with a laugh. 'I'm scared stiff of spiders and practically faint. What's your great fear, Louise?' he asked, turning to the girl, whom he had hardly spoken to all the evening, as he had devoted himself mostly to Jean. 'Men?' he added.

She went red for a moment and then laughed. 'No—mine is blood. Even the slightest scratch makes me feel sick.'

'And you, Peter?' Jean asked, still so angry it was hard to control it. She was sick, too—sick and tired of the way Peter behaved, baiting her, making her look a fool all the time.

He shrugged. 'Frankly—marriage, I suppose. My parents weren't happy, so . . .'

'Yet you got married?' Louise said with a smile.

'I had no choice,' Peter said with a smile, and then he looked at Jean. 'Had I, darling?'

Her mouth was dry with fear. For a moment

141

she had thought he was going to tell them the truth—that it was not a real marriage, that they slept in separate rooms and he only kissed her in public as part of his act.

'So it seems,' she said with a smile that was difficult to make and even harder to keep as Louise laughed.

'How romantic it sounds,' she said.

Well, Jean was thinking unhappily, it might sound romantic, but that was all. In reality it was more of a nightmare, married and yet not married to a man you loved.

CHAPTER EIGHT

It was amazing how quickly the local grapevine worked, Jean found herself thinking the next day. First she had taken the children to school and had done some shopping, decided to return home and then wished she hadn't, because Louise's red sports car was there, parked as usual, but there was no sign of either Louise or Peter. So Jean had driven back to the school early, having a chat with one of the mothers as they waited.

Everything looked beautiful in the welcome sunshine. Already the mud was becoming dry dust, rising in clouds as the huge lorries rumbled along, and the goats seemed to be enjoying their feasts in the freshly green grass. The flowers had ceased to be simply depressed-looking buds and were bright with colour.

'So you're the latest to fall for his charm,' Jean's companion observed with a smile as they walked together towards the school gate. On every side was beauty, Jean was thinking, looking at the distant range of blue mountains, the sudden drop to the dam where already there were small launches careering around with water-skiers racing behind them.

'The latest?' Jean repeated mechanically.

'You know who I mean,' the girl whose name Jean could never remember laughed. 'We all fall for him in turn.'

'You mean Peter?' Jean asked, suddenly on guard. Was it so obvious that she loved her so-called husband?

The girl laughed. 'Ach, man, no. He's your husband. I'm talking about David Fox.'

'David? Oh, yes, David Fox.' Jean laughed. 'What makes you think I fancy him?'

'Well, you were with him yesterday morning and seen at the hotel.'

'We had coffee while he was phoning his mother!'

Laughing, Jean's companion shook her head. 'A likely story! Amazing what he can think up. It's never "come and see my etchings" with David—he thinks of something better.'

'It was just a cup of . . .' Jean began, but the

doors of the school opened and the children came pouring out, shouting as they always did, racing towards the waiting cars, and Jean walked back towards theirs. How right Peter was, she was thinking, as to the gossip here. If you can't have a cup of coffee with a man you know without being involved!

'I'm hungry,' Nick complained as he reached her.

Jean looked down at his eager face. Yes, he was hungry, she thought—hungry for love. Like herself. She took his hand in hers.

'We're driving straight home, Nicky, because I've done all the shopping. Let's run to the car.'

He nodded, and they ran across the ground, getting to the car before the others.

At lunch the second evidence of the speed of the grapevine struck Jean. Louise was with them, chattering away to the children, while Peter watched her, with that sort of amazed look on his face that he always seemed to have when Louise was around. Vanessa turned to Jean.

'Are you really scared of crocodiles? Everyone says so at school.'

Jean closed her eyes for a second. How on earth did they know? Had Amelia been talking? Who else? 'I don't know. I've only seen crocodiles in a zoo and I thought them hideous.'

Peter laughed. 'We'll have to ask Aunt Leila

144

to show Jean her crocs some time, won't we?'

Vanessa laughed. 'That's a good idea, Uncle Peter.'

Later that afternoon Jean was in her bedroom, writing to her mother. This time the letter did not go so smoothly, for she could not forget the way Peter looked at Louise and seemed to act as if there was only Louise in the room with him. Was it her imagination, Jean wondered, but Louise was clever, amusing and beautiful. How could one compete with that?

Dorcas knocked on the door and opened it. 'The master, he say ask to see you,' she said, her plump figure tightly clothed in her pale blue uniform dress with the neatly pleated white apron over it.

'Now?' Jean asked, jumping off the bed where she had been sprawled as she wrote. Dorcas nodded.

'Now, he said.'

Puzzled, Jean hurried to the study, wondering if she should knock, but decided not to as he had sent for her. She opened the door and he was standing by the window, his back towards her.

'Peter . . .' she began.

He turned and she caught her breath with surprise. Never had she seen him looking so angry.

'What's all this I hear about you and David Fox?' he demanded, striding across the room towards her.

145

'Oh no . . .' Jean began.

'I want the truth, Jean. I didn't engage you to flirt with every man in the neighbourhood and have us talked about. We agreed that we would make the marriage appear a happy one, no matter how we felt and now you've messed up everything!' His voice, slow, quiet, was full of fury.

And suddenly she was as angry. 'You would accuse me,' she said. 'But what about you and Louise?'

He looked startled, moving backwards so that he was resting against the long desk which was covered with papers and books.

'I don't see where Louise comes in.'

'You don't?' Jean moved forward angrily. 'Well, I suppose you're more . . . more discreet, or shall I say clever? She spends every day here alone with you, and then you say you don't know where she comes in!'

'Are you suggesting . . .' His voice was cold.

She stood up straight, her hands on her hips. 'Yes, I am suggesting!' she told him 'I often wonder what Luke must think, and as the wretched grapevine works so well, I expect everyone around here knows you're interested in Louise, so what about me? How do you think I like it?'

'Louise spends most of her time with Luke.'

'Is that so?' Jean snapped. 'Then why does she park her car outside our house?'

'And why shouldn't she? Luke is usually up

here at the back, so why should she walk up from his cottage?'

Jean stood still, biting her lower lip. Peter could be right, she thought. Maybe she had been building up something from nothing. All the same . . .

'I had coffee yesterday with David Fox at the hotel while he phoned his mother who's ill,' she persisted.

'Yes, I heard that story, too,' Peter told her.

They were both silent, staring at one another. Jean's anger was leaving her slowly as she realised that Peter could be right and she had imagined it all.

'Peter,' she said, holding out her hands, 'surely just having a cup of coffee with a man doesn't mean I'm in love with him?'

'Tongues here twist the truth—they seem to delight in it. All right,' Peter sighed. 'I'm sorry if I jumped on you, but I don't want anyone to suspect the truth about us—and I'm sure you feel the same?'

She looked up at him, the words inside her fighting to rush out, to tell him the truth, that she loved him as she had never thought it was possible to love anyone . . . but what good would it do her? He would probably be horrified, might even pack her off to England out of the way and employ Louise as a governess-housekeeper!

'Yes, Peter, of course I do,' she managed to say quietly.

147

'Good.' He turned away and went to sit down at his desk. His usual method of dismissal, Jean thought as she left the room.

She stood for a few moments in the corridor near the front of the house, for she could not forget what Peter had said: 'Make it appear a happy marriage no matter how we feel.' How those words hurt her. Surely they meant that already he regretted it and wished that he was free to marry Louise?

Yet perhaps it was foolish to think that, for as the marriage was in name only, it could easily be ended. Or was it the arrogance of his that made him want the local people to know that *he* was the one getting rid of an unwanted wife and that was why he didn't want her name mixed up with David?

David! Of all the men she knew, he was the gentlest, most understanding—even more so than Luke; who was also a darling. Her mind returned to those hurting words: ". . . no matter how we feel", because they hurt most. Why did Peter say them? If only she knew—if she could be sure!

Vanessa came in running through the door from the *stoep*, her eyes excited.

'We've found a crocodile for you, Auntie Jean.' she said. 'Come and see it!'

A crocodile for her, Jean thought. Of all the things she wanted in the world, a crocodile was the last.

'Come on,' Vanessa coaxed. 'It won't bite

you. We won't let it,' she promised.

Nick had come in, too, looking excited. 'Please do come!' he begged.

'All right,' Jean agreed. After all, she wasn't really frightened of crocodiles, because they had never come into her life—nor could she make out why her so-called 'fear' had been built up so much. 'Of course I'll come,' she said gaily.

It was a surprisingly long walk down to the river. Jean had never before been on the wide stone steps that went down the mountainside. Glancing round, she thought what a difference the sunshine made. Now everything looked so clear and fresh—only the river, half hidden by close-growing bushes and trees, looked dirty. The water was no longer turgid but was moving fast, carrying broken branches and leaves on the current that was quick because of the heavy rain and the water falling fast down the many waterfalls and small streams.

Nick was running ahead, looking round excitedly. Was it all right, Jean suddenly wondered, for them to go down alone? Ought she to have told Peter? Somehow she felt like sticking her tongue out at him like a naughty child—why did he think he always had the right?

'Hurry up, Auntie Jean!' Nick called, well ahead of them.

Vanessa walked with Jean. 'Have you talked to Uncle Peter yet about the camping?' she asked.

Jean turned to her. 'I am sorry, Vanessa, I forgot all about it. Who's going with you all?'

Vanessa gave a list of names, many of which Jean recognised. Two adults, parents of one of the children, were going as well, so surely Peter would agree? Yet if he was in one of his moods? Maybe the best person for Vanessa to talk to was Louise! She could no doubt persuade Peter, Jean thought bitterly, half tempted to suggest it to Vanessa.

At last they were on a level with the river. Looking back up the hill, it seemed even longer than it had as they came down. The ground was uneven, outlined with half-covered roots of trees and with bushes covered with prickly thorns. The mosquitoes were buzzing round, too. Nick was beating a bush and just as Jean was going to say that perhaps that wasn't a very wise thing to do, Vanessa cried out, her voice terrified:

'Look out!'

Jean turned round and for a moment, her heart seemed to stand still with fear, for she had nearly trodden on a crocodile whose head emerged from a pile of branches. He was very still, but his eyes bright and menacing.

'I nearly trod on it,' Jean gasped, shocked. 'A good thing you called out!'

Nick came running, his face bright with excitement. 'You really thought it was alive?' He danced about her. 'Auntie Jean, you must be dumb. You really thought it was alive!'

Jean felt as if she had been slapped in the face. She looked at Vanessa. 'It wasn't?'

Vanessa was giggling. She bent down, went close to the crocodile and pulled it out from the bushes. It was only a long flat head, hideous, and lifelike.

'I borrowed it from Auntie Leila. I told her I wanted to show it to you,' she grinned.

Now Jean understood! It was all Peter's doing. He wanted to make her look a fool and had succeeded. He had told Vanessa that they must show Jean one of Auntie Leila's crocodiles. It was all Peter's doing. Why had he to act like this? she wondered. Always cutting her down to size.

Nick was wandering down the path, but Vanessa stepped nearer Jean. 'Are you mad at me? I thought you'd find it funny,' she said anxiously. 'It was only meant as a joke.'

She sounded really upset, so Jean managed to smile. 'I'm sure you did, Vanessa. It just . . . well, it gave me a fright.'

A scream broke the stillness around them. Nick? Another trick, Jean thought.

'Where's Hugh?' she asked.

Vanessa was still looking upset. 'He wouldn't come. He didn't think it was funny He thought you might be scared.'

Now Jean found she could laugh. 'He was right, I was for a moment.'

Another scream broke the stillness. Shriller,

more genuine, Jean thought, suddenly alarmed.

'Where's Nick?' she demanded.

Vanessa pushed past her, running along the faintly marked pathway. She stopped suddenly, her face white with fear.

'He's fallen in the river!' she shouted.

Again Jean hesitated. Were they doing a series of jokes on her? But Vanessa waved frantically. 'It's true, Auntie Jean,' she shouted. 'He's in the river!'

It was true. Nick was in the water up to his neck, clinging with both hands to the roots of trees on the riverside. He was pale with fright and tears rolled down his cheeks.

'Run and get Uncle Peter,' Jean ordered Vanessa, and dropped on her knees, clutching hold of Nick's wrists. 'I'll soon pull you up,' she promised the frightened boy.

It was easier said than done, she soon found. In the end, she was lying down on the ground, her arms aching as she took the weight of Nick, for his hands had let go of the tree roots. The swirl of the river's current dragged at him, and try as she might, Jean could not haul him up.

'Are your feet caught?' she asked, aware of the noisy mosquitoes crawling over her face and which she couldn't fight because she dared not let go of Nick's wrists.

He nodded. 'I can't . . . I can't get free.' He looked over his shoulder. 'There are real crocodiles in here!'

Jean looked at the water flowing swiftly by. The current caused so many ripples that it was hard to know if any were warnings of a crocodile's approach. She felt sick with fear. Suppose one came and grabbed at Nick . . . how could she protect him? Were there any big sticks near her? Yet she was afraid to let go of him—the current might be stronger than she was and sweep him free, carrying him along in this dangerous water.

She tried to calm Nick down by talking to him casually, just as if this sort of thing happened every day but he was growing paler, his eyes wide with terror. It seemed hours before she heard Peter shouting, and then suddenly they were all there—Peter, closely followed by Luke, then Hugh and Louise.

'What the hell . . .' Peter began.

'His feet are caught,' Jean said, her neck stiff as she looked up.

'I'll take over,' Luke told her, and knelt by her side, bent over the river and took hold of Nick's wrists. Slowly Jean unlocked her fingers, stiff with their clutching. She stood up, unsteadily, and felt Louise's arm go round her.

'What a fright for you, Jean,' Louise said. 'You must have been scared stiff!'

Peter was pulling off his safari suit jacket. In a moment he had dived in the river. Jean stood very still, unaware of any curious eyes, as she shook with terror. Suppose there was a crocodile in the river, hiding, low down, swooping forward to grab Peter's legs? She felt sick with fear as Peter vanished under the water, but in a moment his head came up. He shook the water from his face and looked up at Luke.

'He's free now. You can haul him up,' he said, and turned to swim along the bank until it was low enough for him to climb out.

Jean watched him, her heart thudding madly. He was all right . . . he was all right! She wanted to cry and be sick at the same time. She forced herself to look away from Peter as he walked towards them, and looked instead at Nick. Nick was crying, his face white. Louise bent down.

'Think what you'll be able to tell them at school, Nicky,' she said gently. 'What an adventure!'

'We'd better get back to the house,' Peter said sternly. 'You're all right, Nick?'

Nick looked at him quickly, his face worried. 'I'm cold.'

'I bet you are,' Peter said with a quick smile. 'Come on, let's get going. A hot drink and a bath, I suggest, for us both.'

It was a long endless climb up the steps. Luke helped Nick, whose legs seemed to be too heavy for him. Louise walked by Jean, talking casually, helped her now and then, because Jean's legs were absurdly wobbly.

It was a relief to go to her room, to change

out of her muddy, torn jeans and put on a pale green dress and brush her cloud of hair. She was still shaking a little. Peter could have been killed . . . Peter could have been killed . . . the words drummed in her head like a record that wouldn't stop. What would she have done if he had died? How could she have borne it? Suddenly the tears of shock won and she stood in the middle of the room, her hands to her face.

The door quietly opened and Louise's voice startled her.

'Drink this, Jean,' said Louise, handing her a glass. 'It'll burn your throat, but you need it. It must have been one ghastly shock.'

Jean obeyed. The liquid did burn her throat, it seemed to make its way down inside her, leaving a warm path behind.

'It was . . . pretty awful. I was afraid crocodiles would come along.'

'Well, they didn't.' Louise sat on the edge of the bed. 'Sit down, Jean. Your legs must be wobbly.'

Jean obeyed again. 'They are,' she confessed. 'I don't know why.'

'I know,' Louise said with a strange smile. 'I bet your arms ached, hanging on to Nick. You've been bitten a lot.'

'I know. I couldn't hit the beastly things.'

'When you feel well enough, Peter wants to see you . . . not only you but the children as well.'

'Nick must be suffering from shock,' said Jean.

'He is. I've put him to bed and sent for the doctor,' Louise told her.

Jean took a long deep breath. So Louise was taking charge! *She* had put Nick to bed—*she* had sent for the doctor. *She*, too, had come to tell Jean that Peter wanted to see her

'I'm all right, now,' she said, standing up.

Louise smiled. 'Good!'

Peter was waiting on the *stoep*. He had showered and changed into khaki shorts and a white shirt. Vanessa was curled up in a chair, her face frightened. Hugh stood on one side, his face with its old faraway look.

'Ah, sit down, Jean,' Peter said briskly. 'I want to know what you were all doing down there when you know it's forbidden ground?'

There was a silence. Jean glanced at Vanessa. Poor girl—she would be terrified of offending her Uncle Peter, particularly as she wanted to go camping.

'We were looking for crocodiles,' Jean said, her voice casual. She looked across the *stoep*. 'Hugh wasn't with us,' she added.

'I see,' Peter nodded, frowning. 'But why on earth did you take the kids down there? You should know how dangerous it is.'

Suddenly Vanessa began to cry. 'It wasn't her, Uncle Peter. It was me. We got Auntie Leila's crocodile head and . . . and showed it to Auntie Jean. She . . . she thought it was real.'

156

'You didn't?' He turned to look at Jean. He sounded amused.

For the second time that day fury filled her. What right had he to behave as he did? She would be a fool to put up with it.

'I did,' she said calmly, clenching her hands tightly. 'After all, it was your idea, Peter. At lunch you told Vanessa to show me Leila's crocodile, so she did. It was your fault entirely . . .' she was startled to hear her voice rising angrily.

Peter's eyes narrowed as he gazed at her. 'I suppose in a way, it was,' he agreed, as usual surprising her by saying something opposite to what she expected. He turned to Vanessa. 'But it wasn't very nice of you to frighten her.'

'I thought it would be a joke. I didn't know . . . I didn't think,' Vanessa said miserably.

'That last is right. You didn't think. Now what about Nick? How come he fell into the river?'

'He must have slipped. He was so amused because I'd believed it was a live crocodile that he danced away. I'm afraid I didn't miss him at once . . . and when he screamed, I thought it was another trick, and then Vanessa found him and yelled for me and . . . and I sent her up to you.'

'But why did you go down in the first place?' Peter stood in front of her, frowning.

Jean lifted her pointed chin and glared back. 'For one simple reason, Peter Crosby,' she

157

said angrily. 'I'm fed to the teeth the way you make fun of me and make me look an idiot! I knew if I didn't go and see the crocodile that you would be telling everyone about it and they would all laugh at me.' She jumped up and glared at him. 'Don't blame Vanessa for something that was your fault. She'd never have thought of it but for you, and none of this would have happened!' She brushed by him and almost ran to her room, locking the door and flinging herself on the bed.

Why did she love such a man? she asked herself. How could she love someone who seemed to take a delight in making her feel small? Yet she did. Oh yes, she did.

CHAPTER NINE

In the morning, Jean showered and dressed slowly and worriedly, for she was wondering if perhaps, in losing her temper the day before, she had gone too far. Why had she called him *Peter Crosby*—could it have given their secret away? Had she been rude? After all, in Peter's eyes she was simply an employee, as he would put it. The night before she had stayed in her room, still shaking a little, still hugging the pillow. Violet had brought in dinner on a tray, but no one came to see her. Jean had heard a stranger's voice and guessed him to be the doctor she had not yet met. She wondered how Nicky was, but Louise was there, so everything would be all right, Jean thought with this bitterness that was new to her.

If only Louise had never come . . . if only . . . but then life was full of *if onlys*, she reminded herself as she dressed for breakfast.

Hugh and Vanessa were already there, as well as Peter. He looked up with a smile, to Jean's amazement.

'Feeling better?' he asked. 'Must have been a bit of a nightmare yesterday.'

Jean helped herself to the kidneys and bacon waiting on the sideboard. 'That's no lie,' she said with a little laugh. 'Is Nick going to school?'

'No. The doctor advised a day or so at home, though Nick wants to go.' Peter laughed. 'Louise has made him feel a positive hero instead of a young idiot who should know better than to run alongside the river's edge.' He glanced at his watch. 'See you at lunch,' he said, and left the room.

Jean ate as fast as she could, leaving it to Vanessa to talk. Most of the time it was about the camping idea.

'You will talk to Uncle Peter, won't you, Auntie Jean?' she asked.

'Yes, of course . . . when I get the chance,' Jean said.

At the school, she dropped the children and left them to walk across the wide patch before the school while she turned the car and drove away. She was feeling annoyed with the grapevine, because it was ridiculous to say she was having an affair with David just because she had coffee with him at the hotel! Then all the gossip about the crocodiles—goodness knew what was going round at that very moment, passed on from one to another. How everyone must be laughing at her!

She went to the stores and did her shopping, collected the post and drove home. The sun was still shining and everything looked fresh and beautiful. Her first surprise as she reached the farmhouse was that there was no sign of Louise's car—which was a change, but then Peter had said Louise would be looking after Nicky.

Jean went straight to Nicky's bedroom. He was sitting up in bed, carefully drawing a picture. He looked up with a smile.

'The doctor says I'm too ill to go to school,' he said almost proudly. 'But I want to go. It was exciting, wasn't it?'

Jean sat on the edge of the bed, looking round the room he shared with Hugh. It had a bare impersonal look somehow, with white furniture, a green rug on the polished floor and pale green curtains.

'Yes, Nicky, it was exciting,' she said, remembering vividly the horror and fear in her mind as she clung to his wrists, wondering what she would do if a crocodile did come.

'I bet I'm the only one at school who's had an adventure like that,' he said proudly.

Jean smiled. 'Well, please don't have another one, because I didn't find it much fun.'

Nicky's face sobered. 'Auntie Louise said you saved my life, Auntie Jean. Thank you.' The solemn, rather pompous way he spoke those last words made her eyes smart.

She put out her hand and took hold of his. 'Let's thank God,' she said, 'for taking care of us.'

She heard the phone bell ringing and hurried to answer it.

It was a strange feminine voice. 'I wish to speak to Mr. Crosby.' She spoke in an aggressive way as if implying that Jean might try to stop her from speaking to Mr. Crosby.

'I'll get him. Who is it speaking?' Jean asked. 'Tell him Miranda and he'll understand,' the unknown person said, even more aggressively.

'I will,' Jean promised.

But Peter wasn't in his study. She hurried through the house and saw that his car had gone from the garage. She hurried back.

'I'm afraid he's not in . .'

'You certainly took your time about finding that out,' the voice complained. 'All right. I may be off to Rhodesia right away, but I'll give him a ring when I come back.' There was a click as the receiver was replaced and Jean put down her phone.

Who could Miranda be—and why had she sounded so . . . so bossy? That was another thing, Jean reminded herself, that she must ask Peter when he came in: first, the camping holiday Vanessa wanted to go on, and now a phone call from someone called Miranda.

As she drank coffee on the *stoep*, Jean's mind kept returning again and again to Peter. Where had he gone? Why hadn't he said anything at breakfast about being out? He usually did, in case there were phone calls. And where was Louise? At least they weren't together, because if they had been, they would have only taken one car.

She spent the rest of the morning with Nick, playing games and feeling glad that the traumatic experience, as Louise had called it, didn't seem to have upset him at all. Then Jean drove to the school to fetch the children. This time she couldn't avoid the others waiting for their children and they crowded round her, saying:

'Is it true . . . ?' 'Was there a crocodile there?' 'Weren't you scared?' 'A good thing you were there with them.'

Jean was relieved when the children came running and they could drive home. Peter was still out and there was no sign of Louise, so they ate their lunch and Vanessa went to her room to get her homework done while Hugh went outside to find Luke. He came back to say Luke wasn't there.

'Where can he be?' Hugh asked.

Jean shrugged. 'I haven't a clue. I don't know where Uncle Peter is either, or Auntie Louise. Everyone seems to have vanished.'

Hugh smiled. 'Well, we're here, anyway.'

She smiled back. 'Yes, Hugh, we're here,' she said. 'You wouldn't go and play with Nicky, would you? I don't want him to get bored, because . . . '

'Then he might start to think? He could have died, Auntie Jean. Thanks for saving him,' said Hugh, his eyes thoughtful. 'You really love us, don't you?'

'Of course I do.' She moved quickly, hugging him, kissing him lightly on the cheek. 'So does Uncle Peter,' she added.

Hugh nodded. 'I'm glad,' he said. 'I'll go and play with Nicky.'

Jean was in the larder, making a note of what was missing, for Violet had a habit of waiting until the last leaf of tea had gone and would then come and say sadly: 'No tea, no tea at all, *nkosikas*,' with a solemn voice, and then Peter would be furious, saying Jean should have kept a check on everything, when Vanessa came running.

'Uncle Peter's come and he's got someone with him. Maybe it's Gran!'

Jean followed more slowly and reached the *stoep* just as Peter and his companion came in.

'Maggie!' Jean gasped.

'Jeanie!' Maggie smiled as they went into

each other's arms.

'What on earth are . . .?'

'What am I doing here?' Maggie stood back, laughing a little but looking years older with dark bags under her eyes and her hair lank, so different from the Maggie Jean remembered.

'What about a drink?' suggested Peter, leading the way to the lounge. 'I could do with one, and I'm sure Maggie could. It was quite a drive. We got caught up behind about five of those huge containers and the dust . . . eh, Maggie?' He turned from the bamboo bar in the corner of the room.

'It was pretty awful,' she agreed, pulling off her coat and sinking into a chair. 'It's so hot here . . .' She smiled at Jean 'Don't look so stunned.'

'Vanessa thought it was your mother, Peter.'

Peter carefully carried the glass to Maggie. 'She's still in Durban, can't seem to make up her mind. One day she wants to go back to London, the next she has made so many friends in Durban, she just doesn't know what to do.' He smiled at Maggie. 'I'll leave you in Jean's hands. See you later.'

'Thanks a ton, Peter,' Maggie said with a smile. Vanessa had vanished, so Jean and Maggie were alone.

'It's lovely to see you,' Jean began, 'but I thought . . .'

'So did I.' Maggie's voice lost its life, becoming dull. 'So did he, and then he changed his mind. Just before the wedding. He just walked out, writing me a note.'

'What a . . .'

'Maybe I should have seen it coming. He hates responsibilities. It was all right while we were engaged, but marriage—! Apparently it scared him stiff. I suddenly hated England, London and my parents. They were good. No one said, "I told you so", but they'd never liked Jock and I could feel them thinking "Well, we warned her. Better now than later," so I thought I'd come out and see how you were getting on.'

Jean smiled ruefully. 'Not very well. There's a girl called Louise . . .'

'Oh yes, Peter was talking about her on the way here. Seems she's pretty wonderful.'

'She is, indeed! Smashingly gorgeous, brilliantly clever, witty, good with the children and just . . .'

'What Peter wanted? But hasn't he found it in you? I mean, he doesn't know that I know, but is it still . . .?' Maggie hesitated for a moment.

Jean laughed, her eyes sad. 'Yes, it is still. Separate rooms, and I don't even have to lock the door. Just no interest in me.' She sighed. 'Maybe I was a fool to come out, to ever dream . . .'

'I don't agree. We couldn't live without dreams. At least we've enjoyed them even if they don't work out as we want. Already

I'm getting over Jock. It still hurts like mad, because I'm fiendishly jealous and I hate to think of him with another girl, yet at the same time I'm beginning to realise there are other fish in the sea. By the way, we stopped at the hotel before coming here and I met a real eye-smasher—David somebody or other. Peter said you fancied him.'

'Of course I don't! David is a darling, but ... but ...'

'He isn't Peter.' Maggie stood up. 'Could I have a shower and unpack? Peter says I can stay as long as I like.'

'But how did he know you were coming?' asked Jean.

'I rang up from Johannesburg this morning. You'd gone with the children to school. Peter said he'd pick me up at the airport. The plane was late, so we had lunch on the way back.' Maggie picked up her coat. 'He's quite a nice guy when you talk to him alone,' she said, looking round her. 'How do you like this sort of life? Seems smashing to me, but I'm wondering if I wouldn't get awfully bored.'

Jean led the way to the bathroom, thinking how lucky they had a small spare room that was seldom used.

'I just don't have time to be bored,' Jean said. 'I help Luke sometimes, or rather I check for Peter.'

'Luke? Who's Luke?' Maggie asked, turning on them both, looking up with a smile. 'Sounds like there are men around to help me rebuild my ego.'

'Luke manages the farm for . . . for Peter.' She had nearly said *us*, because that was how she thought of it, but of course she had no right to think like that. 'See you later, so don't hurry,' Jean said, leaving her.

Peter came out of his study and beckoned her.

'We must try to cheer her up,' he said, 'so how about phoning to ask David and Luke, and of course Louise, to dinner?'

Jean looked up at the tall man who always towered above her and wondered why he bothered with Maggie's problems.

'I'd no idea Maggie was coming,' she told him.

'I know—she told me. Of course it's all right for her to come out. We've got room and it's company for you. I'm busy, so will you phone?'

'Sure,' said Jean, and watched the study door close as he went back into his room.

She walked to the kitchen to look in the deep-freeze. Was there time to thaw something? Why had Peter said: 'and of course Louise'? Why was it *of course*? In any case, where was Louise? The same applied to Luke. Both of them had vanished that day—were they together?

Maggie found Jean in the kitchen and stood amazed. 'What on earth are you doing?' she demanded.

167

jean, busy, looked up. 'I'm making a casserole for tonight, also a mousse with strawberries.'

'I thought you had domestic staff. My,' Maggie giggled, 'doesn't that sound posh?'

'We have, two very good ones, but it's Dorcas's day off, and though Violet can cook simple things like scrambled eggs, we're having a dinner party tonight to welcome you, so I thought I'd better get cracking.'

Maggie leant against the kitchen wall, her arms folded.

'You've learned a lot,' she commented.

Jean added some sherry to the casserole and put on the glass lid before looking up with a smile. 'Peter's a great one for inviting guests at the last moment, so I've had to learn,' she explained.

Maggie glanced round. 'I don't think much of the house. Somehow I imagined it would be very . . . well, with it, if you know what I mean.'

Jean washed her hands. 'Well, this was never Peter's. It was his sister's and her husband's, and they didn't have much money. Mind, they did, but he spent it all on the farm.'

'But Peter won't want to live here for the rest of his life? What'll happen to it then?'

Turning round, Jean looked pale. 'That's what I often wonder. He's got this commission for the books, but when that's finished . . . yet he feels his responsibilities as the children's guardian very strongly and he thinks this farm should be kept for them.'

'But I don't want to farm,' a quiet voice said.

It was Hugh who had come in unseen, his face showing how troubled he was.

'This is Auntie Maggie,' Jean said. 'This is Hugh. Why don't you tell Uncle Peter you don't want to farm, Hugh? He's thinking of you mostly.'

'Will you tell him?' Hugh asked. 'He listens to you. That's what Vanessa says.'

'Yes, I'll tell him,' said Jean, hoping she would remember it. Now what had she to remember first? —Vanessa and her camping holiday, then that woman who phoned and was called Miranda; and now Hugh who didn't want to farm. She would have to be alone with Peter, and how rarely that happened.

In any case, she realised with a jolt, if they sold the farm and the children returned to England where they were born, would Peter need a wife, 'for convenience only'?

CHAPTER TEN

It proved to be a difficult task, finding Louise to invite her. Jean had a chat with Louise's aunt, who sounded irritable.

'How do I know where she is?' she asked. 'She never tells us anything. Always was difficult, that girl. Never listens to what you say. Can I take a message?'

'Yes, would you tell her that Jean's got a visitor, a friend from England, and that we're giving her a welcoming party tonight and would like Louise to join us,' Jean said carefully, having heard quite a lot about Louise's aunt, who should have lived in the Victorian age.

Luke was even harder to contact and it wasn't until late in the afternoon that Hugh found him, looking at one of the cows.

'I was on the lands,' Luke said as he came in and was introduced to Maggie. 'Sorry if you were looking for me. Yes, thanks, I never say no to one of Jean's dinners,' he added with a smile, then seemed to hesitate. 'Who's coming?'

'David,' said Jean 'Louise, if I can get her.'

'Isn't she at home?' Luke sounded surprised. 'She usually goes back about this time.'

'I left a message.'

He grinned. 'Then she'll be here all right. Can't keep our little Louise away, can we?' he said, and walked away.

Maggie whistled softly. 'Rather dishy. You fancy him?'

Jean laughed. 'I like him, but . . .'

'As I said before, he's not Peter.' Maggie was sprawled on the floor, stretched out on a rug, looking much happier than when she had arrived, her hair brushed back and twisted round her head, her long thin dress of purple voile pleating round her slim body. 'Now don't forget David.'

'I'm getting him now. At least, I'm trying,' said Jean, taking up the phone. It took quite a while to get through to the Research Station, but at last she got to David.

'Come to dinner?' David said. 'Fine, I'd love to.' He chuckled. 'I rather wondered if I was in Peter's bad books, but when I saw him today, he seemed quite friendly.'

Jean laughed a little. 'You mean about us having coffee together? I was mad at them.'

'Take no notice, my dear. You'll get used to it as you do to everything in this beautiful land. See you later, then.'

Sighing with relief, Jean came to sit by Maggie's side.

'That's that, and I shan't mind if Louise doesn't come,' she said.

'You jealous?'

Jean smiled ruefully. 'I've always been against jealousy, saying you should trust the one you love, but it doesn't work in real life. Peter thinks so much of Louise, he's always talking about her, as you said, always praising her, and he just stares at her as if . . . as if someone had knocked him on the head and he hadn't recovered. You'll see . . . that is, if she comes tonight.'

'What has she got that you haven't?' Maggie stretched her arms happily, twisting her body

171

about. 'Gosh, that bath was welcome! Tell me, then.'

'I should think just about everything,' Jean said miserably. 'She's been to agricultural college, so she can advise on farming; she's taught children, so she knows how to handle them. She's also beautiful, witty, charming and a darling.'

'A darling?' Maggie was startled.

Jean told her about the incident with the crocodile, the danger to Nicky, and even more so to Peter, the sympathetic way Louise had helped Jean afterwards.

'She sounds smashing,' Maggie said thoughtfully. 'Now we must find a way to make you better in every respect. We can't let her take your Peter.'

'*My* Peter . . .' mused Jean. 'Fat chance I have of ever having Peter as mine!' She stood up slowly. 'I'm going to shower and change Might as well make the best of things,' she added with a smile. 'Be seeing you.'

'Sure,' Maggie waved her hand. 'I'll probably fall asleep.'

But three-quarters of an hour later, Jean came back, and Maggie was certainly not asleep. She was perched on the arm of the couch, her purple voile dress hanging in soft folds round her long, beautiful legs, a glass in one hand, her eyes sparkling like diamonds as she talked, glancing from Peter to Luke and then back to Peter. Peter was staring at her

172

thoughtfully, his chin resting on his hand. Jean stood in the doorway, conscious of her own clumsiness, her height that was too much for a girl, and wondering what she looked like in the long green silk dress that she had made for the family ball.

Maggie looked up. 'Hi there, Jeannie. That colour suits you fine. Doesn't it, Peter?'

Jean felt her cheeks burning as Peter looked at her. A casual amused look. 'It does,' he said, and turned back to Maggie.

So much for the time she had taken to makeup, to brush her hair back from her face and twist it round her head, Jean thought. He hadn't even noticed that she had changed her hair-style!

A car roared up the hill—a red sports car.

'Louise!' Peter exclaimed, his voice bright with pleasure. 'I'll let her in.'

'No, I will,' Jean said, for she was near the screened door that led to the *stoep*. She opened it and Louise came in, looking lovelier than ever in a golden silk dress, long, clinging to the slender body, making her hair look lovelier than usual as it hung down her back.

'Louise, come in,' Peter invited, holding out both his hands. 'You look delectable, delicious and . . .'

'Deplorable?' Louise asked. 'That's what my aunt called me earlier. Thanks for the invitation, Peter.' She looked round the room. 'I think I know everyone here, but . . .' Her gaze reached Maggie.

'Maggie, an old friend of Jean's,' Peter introduced. 'This is Louise, Maggie.'

'So I gathered,' said Maggie, in a rather odd voice.

Soon the party was in full swing, drinking, then going to the dining-room where Violet was moving round, making sure everything was all right. The casserole after prawn cocktails was delicious.

'Nice work, Jeanie,' Maggie said, and looked at Peter. 'I didn't know Jean could cook so well.'

'Dorcas does most of it,' he said casually.

'But she's out today.'

'Is she?' he asked as if not interested, and turned to Louise who was on his other side.

Maggie looked across the table at Jean, who shrugged her shoulders and turned to Luke, who was next to her.

It was a pleasant evening, with plenty to talk about and a friendly atmosphere. Jean had never seen Louise so happy, she was positively glowing with happiness—as if she was in love and something wonderful had happened.

Had Peter told Louise the truth about the marriage that wasn't one? Jean wondered. Was that why Louise was so happy? Had Peter told her that he could easily get rid of Jean and then they could marry and live happily ever after?

'Penny for them, Jean,' David interrupted

174

her thoughts.

There was a sudden silence, the kind that sometimes happens in a crowd, Jean realised unhappily. What could she say?

'I was just thinking,' she said hastily.

'About what?'

She looked round the room and saw they were all gazing at her, waiting for an answer. She thought wildly and then told the truth.

'I was wondering why Louise looked so happy.' There was a roar of laughter as everyone turned to Louise. For once, she was looking embarrassed.

'Do I? Well, this is a nice party. I mean . . .'

Peter jumped up as if rescuing her from an awkward situation.

'I could do with another drink. Who would like one?' he asked, and that changed the slant of the conversation.

It was a very pleasant party, as Maggie said the next day as she sat by Jean's side and they took the children to school. Nicky was with them, looking very pleased with himself and Jean thought how lucky they were he could see the happening like that and not be frightened because of it.

More introductions had to be made to the other mothers dropping their children at school and a lot of invitations so that the morning flew by. As they went to fetch the children, Maggie said thoughtfully:

'Know something, Jeanie? I think I could be

happy here. It's a much friendlier atmosphere than I expected, and it's so very beautiful.'

'Yes. David always says you either love or hate this place.'

'And you? Do you love or hate it?'

'I love it, but . . .'

Maggie turned in the seat and looked at her. 'Only because Peter is here. Right? Poor Jean, it is tough on you.'

'You saw what I meant about Louise? I mean, the way Peter looks at her.'

'I didn't notice that, but I did see the way he jumped to rescue her when you said she looked so happy Funny how upset she was. I mean, after all, it's something of a compliment, isn't it?'

'I thought she looked smashing,' Jean said as she drove towards the long white gate outside the school yard and parked the car.

'I liked her. I couldn't help it,' Maggie admitted.

Jean laughed. 'So do I. We can't blame her for it all—I mean, if Peter has fallen in love with her . .' Jean's voice dwindled away miserably. 'In a way, I'd rather know, but until I do, I can still . . .'

'Hope,' Maggie supplied the word. 'What would we do without hope? When I heard from Jock, I still hoped. I rang and rang him until his mother got quite unpleasant and said she'd have to have the phone cut off if I went on being such a pest. I suppose I was, but then you see I thought I loved him. . You don't just think you love Peter?'

Jean smiled ruefully. 'I'm afraid not. I was almost certain, and when he was in that river, diving to rescue Nicky, and I was afraid a crocodile would slide up silently and catch hold of Peter,' she shivered, 'I knew then that I loved him beyond any shadow of doubt.'

The children came in their groups and they drove back to the house. Louise's car was parked outside as usual, Jean noticed. Maybe she was staying for lunch. She was!

That evening David invited them to dinner at the hotel as he lived alone and said he wasn't good at entertaining.

The next day, Jean and Maggie went out to coffee all the morning, finishing up in the stores, looking at the beautifully coloured squares of material.

It was at lunch that they were all startled. Peter was in one of his cheerful good-tempered moods—though he always was when Louise was there, Jean was thinking—when suddenly Peter said:

'I had a letter from Gran today. She's going back to London to live.'

Vanessa looked up. 'She is? How smashing! I wish we were.'

'So do I,' Hugh said quietly.

'London?' said Nicky. 'I'd like to go to London, too.'

'Maybe you'll be able to go and stay with

Gran,' Louise said.

Vanessa looked at her scornfully. 'That isn't the same as living there.'

Peter frowned. 'Look, you kids, let's get this straight. I thought you liked living *here*—that this was your home, your way of living. I . . . we only came out here because we thought you'd be happier.'

'We were hoping you'd be in England and we could come to you,' Vanessa said, her eyes almost accusing as she stared at her uncle.

'But there's the farm . . .'

'I don't want the farm,' said Hugh. He looked at Jean. 'You didn't tell him?'

'I'm sorry, Hugh. I meant to, but I forgot.'

'Tell me what?' Peter asked, frowning.

Hugh took a deep breath and faced his uncle. 'I don't want to farm, Uncle. I've seen how tough it is. You can work hard all the year round and then the hail comes along and your year's work is washed out. That isn't the way I want to live. I'm going to be an architect and see the world.'

'That's what you want to do?' Peter said slowly.

'That's what I'm going to do,' Hugh corrected him.

'I'm going to be a model,' Vanessa announced. 'It would be much easier for me if I lived in London. I mean, up here no one has a chance of getting a really smashing sort of a job.'

'And you, Nicky?' Peter asked.

Nick was eating his ice cream. 'I'm going to work in a zoo,' he said. 'I like animals.'

'I see. Well, we'll have to look into this,' Peter said slowly. 'There's only one thing. If we go back to England, you'll probably all have to go to boarding school—my job takes me round the world lecturing. How would you like that?'

Vanessa clapped her hands. 'Smashing, Uncle, just smashing, then we can fly out in the hols and stay with you and Auntie Jean. That would be absolutely great!'

Hugh nodded. 'It would give me a chance to study the architecture of different countries.'

'I could have a camera and take photos of the wild animals,' Nick dreamed aloud happily.

'Well,' Peter said, and smiled at them, 'you certainly have got me thinking. Nothing can be done in a hurry, but we'll look into it.'

'Peter,' said Jean, 'while I've got the chance there's something else.'

'So what?' he asked, looking at her, his eyes narrowed.

Was he, she wondered, already planning how to get rid of her because in England there would be no need to have a wife of convenience?

'There's going to be a camping holiday soon, and Vanessa . . .' Jean began, but he interrupted.

'Wants to go? Why not? Quite a few adults are going.' He turned to Maggie. 'Are you fond of camping? David is going.'

Maggie's eyes sparkled. 'It sounds fun.'

'Good, then go ahead, Vanessa.'

The girl jumped up and ran to hug him.

'You really are the sweetest!' she said, and then turned to hug Jean. 'So are you, Auntie Jean, the very sweetest,' she finished, and danced out of the room, going straight to the phone to tell her friends the good news.

*   *   *

Jean was alone, drinking coffee when she heard the car. Vanessa had gone with her group of friends camping and Peter had driven Maggie to the hotel where she was to meet David and he would drive her to the Falls. Peter had just returned, vanishing into his study after hesitating on the *stoep* as if there was something he wished to talk to Jean about and then had changed his mind. Jean was wondering what it was Peter had been about to say when the car drew up. She got up to see who it was, expecting it to be Louise.

But it wasn't. A long white car was parked outside and out stepped a tall thin woman in a green trouser suit, her hair piled high on her head. She looked at the house and then around her, then she came to the door. Jean opened it and the woman looked at her.

'I want to see Mr Crosby,' she said.

Jean immediately recognised the voice.

180

It was Miranda! The awful part was, Jean realised, that she had forgotten to tell Peter that Miranda had phoned.

'Won't you come in and sit down?' Jean asked, holding back the door. 'Then I'll get Peter.'

'Peter?' Miranda echoed as she walked in, looked round critically and then sat down. 'Don't tell me you're his wife?'

'Yes, I am.' Jean stood stiffly, waiting for what might come. It proved to be far worse than she had expected, for a strange smile drifted over Miranda's face. 'I see. You're the girl who got the job and he had to marry you because of the gossip. Right?'

Jean felt herself shiver as if a cold finger had gone down her back. What was she to say?

'I'll get Peter . . .' she began.

'Wait a moment, I've a few things to talk to you about. First, I can't understand why you wanted such a job?'

'Because . . .' Jean began, and paused. Perhaps Peter would want her to say nothing, to refuse to answer.

Miranda looked round. 'Thanks be I didn't come here after all. What a ghastly place! A tin roof—a mess of a house . . . right up here where it can be cold,' she said scornfully. 'What a ghastly place!' she repeated.

'It's a very pleasant place,' Jean said quickly. 'Plenty of room, a lovely view. We like it.'

'We? The wife of convenience,' the woman

181

sneered. 'Does the grapevine know yet?' she asked. 'I'll bet they'll have a laugh!'

'Who are you anyway?' Jean asked, suddenly annoyed with herself for standing there meekly.

'I'm Peter's cousin. He asked me to come and stay with him here and help him with the children. I couldn't make up my mind, and when I decided to help him out—he'd sounded really distressed—he told me he no longer needed me. The next I heard from his mother was that he was married to a very young girl. I put two and two together, looked up the newspapers just before I'd phoned him and saw the advertisement.' She laughed. 'What on earth made you do such a thing? Marriage of convenience!' she said sarcastically. 'Of Peter's convenience, I don't doubt.'

'Hullo, Miranda,' Peter interrupted, his voice amused as he walked into the room. He looked at Jean. 'Leave us alone, Jean,' he said, and she was only too glad to obey him, hurrying to her room, leaning against the door, trying to make sense out of what was happening. Why was Peter's cousin so malicious? Would she tell everyone about it? How would Peter handle her? Was it true that she had agreed to help him, but if so . . .

She curled up on the bed, trying to remember that first interview with Peter. She had not been there long when a phone call he was expecting came through . . . Now, thinking hard, she remembered he had gone into the other room for the first call, yet taken the second call in the room where he was interviewing her. It hadn't made sense.

She wondered what to do. Glancing at her watch, she saw she should be fetching Hugh and Nicky soon from Leila's where they were playing with her children. She went out into the lounge and saw that the white car had gone. She knew a moment of relief and then wondered what it had meant. Had Peter convinced Miranda that it was a real marriage . . . or was she in Manbina, telling everyone the joke?

Peter stood up and Jean jumped. She had not seen him sitting there He came towards her with a smile.

'I've been waiting for you,' he told her.

'I thought . . . I didn't know what . . . That woman!' She shivered.

Peter laughed. 'She's quite a character. Jealous as can be, loathes being rejected, which is what she said I did to her after she had made the important decision of coming to help me with the children.'

'She said she phoned you.'

'Quite right, she did. You may remember I went into the other room? I guessed she'd be annoyed after having been asked to help, and then being told she wasn't wanted.'

'But . . .' Jean looked at him worriedly. 'I don't understand, You'd only just begun to talk to me. You couldn't have known that you were going to . . . to engage me.'

'That's where you're wrong,' he said with a smile. 'As soon as I saw you, I knew you were the one I wanted.'

'But . . . but I don't understand.' Unthinkingly, Jean moved forward, her hand on the back of a chair. 'Why?'

'Isn't that the most stupid question of the year?'

'You're always saying I'm stupid . . .' she began, but he had moved fast and she found herself in his arms, looking up into his face that was suddenly close.

'Look, Jeannie, wasn't it the same with you? Maggie told me this morning that the real reason you took the job was that you'd fallen in love with me when you saw me on the television.' He laughed. 'And I fell in love with you when you walked into the room. It was as simple as that.'

'But . . .' she began.

He laughed, his arms tightening round her. 'I know. *But . . . but* . . . My mother said the same when I told her. "But you don't know her." I expect that's what Maggie said to you. Right? Yet it can happen, as we both know.'

'You mean you really love me?' she said gravely.

'I most certainly do,' he said with equal solemnness.

'But Louise . . . I thought you and Louise . . .'

His arms tightened more round her as he laughed. 'You must be joking! Louise is a darling, but she isn't my type. In any case, she was already in love with Luke.'

'Luke?' Jean gasped. 'I never thought for one moment that . . .'

Peter chuckled. 'It seems that last year she came up and met Luke. They fell in love, but then trouble began. She's the only child of a wealthy man and Luke is just a farm manager. He said he wouldn't marry her until he owned a farm. She came back and made him realise he loved her too much, so he's married her. She's been working on him—proved money doesn't matter. They did it quietly because they knew her family might fuss and she wanted it a quiet happy wedding.'

'They're married?' Jean echoed, still feeling dazed. Louise and Luke?

'The day Maggie arrived. Remember you couldn't find Luke? They'd gone off to Kopstal to be married. They're off tomorrow to tell her parents, but when Luke comes back I'm going to suggest he buys this farm off me over a long period. So he *will* have a farm of his own. As we don't want the money in a lump sum it'll work. We'll invest it for the children to get when of age.'

'Why, that's marvellous, Peter!' Jean stared at him and shook her head. 'I still can't believe it. Why didn't you tell me you loved me? I mean, at the beginning.'

'How was I to know how you'd react? I mean, you meet a girl and in ten minutes propose to her—it sounds daft. You were obviously anti-marriage and ultra-sensitive, I mean, because your attitude towards your family worried me. I thought if I rush things you would turn and run away. This method gave us a chance to know one another and to find out if we would be happy together. I think we would be. What do you say?'

She put up her hand and gently stroked his cheek.

'I can't believe it! It's too wonderful to be true.'

'Perhaps this will help,' he said, his mouth against hers. Her arms tightened round his neck as she closed her eyes. Her dream had come true. It really had.

Much later that evening as they sat in the lounge, talking, they heard a noise. Turning, they saw Nick coming into the room, eyes tightly shut, arms outstretched. Peter jumped up from the couch where he had been sitting with Jean in his arms.

'Something wrong, Nicky?' he asked.

Nicky opened his eyes and stared round him. 'Where am I? How did I get here? I must be walking in my sleep.' He looked up at his uncle with an innocent smile. 'Maybe, Uncle, I should have a room of my own like

Auntie Jean.'

Peter was obviously trying not to smile. 'That can be arranged, Nicky. Tomorrow you can have Auntie Jean's bedroom all to yourself.'

'And Auntie Jean?' Nicky looked across the room to where Jean was sitting, leaning forward, fascinated.

'Auntie Jean no longer walks in her sleep, so we're moving tonight into the big bedroom.'

'And I can have hers? Oh, goody, goody!' Nicky smiled happily.

'Yes indeed,' said Peter, glancing at Jean with a smile. 'It's a good thing, isn't it, darling?'

Jean laughed. 'Yes, a very good thing,' she agreed.

'How about an early night?' said Peter. Nicky had run away happily, skipping as he went. 'We've wasted so much time,' Peter said as he took Jean in his arms. 'Have I told you lately, my darling,' he said quietly as he kissed her, 'that I love you? There's only one thing that troubles me. In my profession, I have to go to some strange places. Will you mind?'

Jean laughed, 'I don't mind where you go so long as we're together.'

He kissed her. 'Don't worry, I'll see to that,' he promised. 'What was it Leila said? Something about a palace of gold?'

'Love converts the hut into a palace of gold,' Jean said, and laughed, her arms tightening round his neck. 'I think she's right, too.'